Sherlock Holmes – A Study in Illustrations

A Collection of Early Illustrations from various publications

Volume 4

The illustrations become more recent, and a fewer number remain out of copyright, but we shall persevere, and we still have some little gems in this volume particularly Gaston Simoes da Fonseca.

Michael J. Foy

Paperback ISBN 978-1-80424-076-2

Published by MX Publishing
335 Princess Park Manor, Royal Drive,
London, N11 3GX
www.mxpublishing.com

Cover design by Brian Belanger

Foreword

We are up to Volume 4 already and just like Dorothy returning to Kansas from Oz, we leave the colourful images of Volume 3 and come back to Monochrome in this book, but don't despair, we have a very cosmopolitan mix of talent from around the world with American, French, Czech, British, and Australian artists included. You will notice, once again a difference in image quality between book illustrations and those that appeared in newspapers.

We start with the Brazilian-born, French Illustrator Gaston Simoes da Fonseca, you may remember 3 of his covers were included in Volume 3, well now we complete his work with these additional 128 images, which were used to illustrate three French books. I must admit that he is one of my favourite illustrators.

Next, we have the 100 illustrations from the Czech born Josef Friedrich, many of his drawings looking very similar to Sidney Paget ones, but they are not straight copies, it's like he chose a different camera angle. Friedrich illustrated three Czech books.

We next have a small contribution of 6 images by French Solar D'alba, whose work was printed in a French newspaper hence the quality isn't that wonderful.

Then American Charles Raymond Macauley illustrated each of the 13 stories in a 1905 edition of the Return of Sherlock Holmes.

Australian John Richard Flanagan illustrated two stories for Collier's magazine in 1924, taking over from Frederic Dorr Steele, (who had illustrated 17 previous ones, the last appearing in the magazine back in 1917. These would be the last Sherlock Holmes stories to appear in Collier's, with Steele's work later returned in other publications, it's as if Doyle preferred to be printed where Steele illustrated.) Of course, you would know all about FDS, if you had Volume 3.

At this point, the next four illustrators share a common publication, namely The San Francisco Call magazine, which in 1905 published 25 sherlock Holmes short stories, using images from Stanley E. Armstrong(8), R Thomson(5), Reginald Gordon Russom(3) & Walter W. Francis(10), so we have these artists grouped together.(And before anyone says 8+5+3+10 adds up to 26, Armstrong and Francis shared the illustration duty on one of the stories, so get your Venn diagrams out.

American Joseph Clement Coll, more famous for illustrating other Sir Arthur Conan Doyle stories, did include one image of Sherlock Holmes as part of a montage of Doyle's work.

20 drawings by Pierre Georges Dutriac are shown next for the thirteen stories found in the Case-Book of Sherlock Holmes which was published from 1921.

This book now goes to the dogs, in the shape of two artist who illustrated that Baskerville Canine, firstly B. Widman produced thirteen Hound of the Baskervilles drawings, when the story was serialized in the St. Louis Republic newspaper in 1902 and then five years later, Paul Henri Thiriat illustrated a French serialized version.

Englishmen Henry Matthew Brock and Joseph William Simpson joined the ranks of Sherlock Holmes illustrators to be found in the Strand Magazine, when they produced drawing for the Red Circle in 1911. (For completeness the Strand Magazine illustrators were, Sidney Paget(38), Arthur Twidle(2), Gilbert Holiday(1), Brock and Simpson(1), as mentioned above, Alec Ball(1), Walter Paget(1)(brother of Sidney), Frank Wiles(4), Alfred Gilbert(3), Howard K. Elcock(7)

Last, but by no means least, we have Arthur Ignatius Keller, an unusual middle name, I suppose, certainly today, but let us not forget Sherlock Holmes was written by Sir Arthur Ignatius Conan Doyle.

There is certainly a very European feel to this volume, with contributions from Gaston Simoes da Fonseca, Josef Friedrich, Stanley E. Armstrong,

Alexis Barquin as usual has helped tremendously with the compilation of this book, and you really must visit his Sir Arthur Conan Doyle website at www.arthur-conan-doyle.com for all things Doyley or is that Doyly.

I also have to thank Aleš Kolodrubec for supplying the images from his copy of the 1907 Mstitel book (A Study in Scarlet), thus completing the Josef Friedrich collection.

Feedback is ALWAYS welcome, and changes are made when I screw things up, which happens regularly.

Anyway, enjoy the fourth volume and number five is going to be another colour one.

Time for another Emerson, Lake, and Palmer Quote,

“Welcome back my friends to the show that never ends, we’re so glad you could attend come inside, come inside.”

Let the show begin.

Mike Foy.

please contacted me at SherlockHolmesImages@gmail.com
or I can be found hanging around in the Sherlock Holmes – A Study in Illustrations Facebook group.

Index

Gaston Simoes da Fonseca

Gastão Simões da Fonseca (or Gaston Simoes da Fonseca)

Born 16th October 1874 in Brazil.

Died 18th June 1943 in France.

A Brazilian-born French artist.

Between 1909 and 1913, he did 131 illustrations for Arthur Conan Doyle stories.

He illustrated Sherlock Holmes in three publications by Félix Juven

- Les Premières Exploits de Sherlock Holmes (1909, Félix Juven)
- Premières Aventures de Sherlock Holmes (1909, Félix Juven)
- Nouvelles Aventures de Sherlock Holmes (1909, Félix Juven)

The two 'Premières' books contained some of the same Sherlock Holmes stories, but with a different number of illustrations in each edition.

I think this table will help explain which stories are illustrated and how many appeared in each book.

Most images had accompanying French text that helped explain the reference (with an English translation in brackets), but for some of the others, I have added my own caption to explains the image.

The image count starts at 4 because the first three were included in Volume 3. The images are shown in Canon story order and have been taken from

- Les Premiers Exploits de Sherlock Holmes (1909, Félix Juven) (PE)
- Premières Adventures de Sherlock Holmes (1909, Félix Juven) (PA)
- Nouvelles Aventures de Sherlock Holmes (1909, Félix Juven) (NA)

	No.	1	2	3	4	5	6	7	8
SCAN	8	PA	PA	PA	PA	PA	PA	PA	PA
REDH	8	NA	NA	NA	NA	NA	NA	NA	NA
IDEN	7	NA	NA	NA	NA	NA	NA	NA	
BOSC	7	NA	NA	NA	NA	NA	NA	NA	
FIVE	8	NA	NA	NA	NA	NA	NA	NA	NA
TWIS	7	NA	NA	NA	NA	NA	NA	NA	
BLUE	8	PE/PA	PE/PA	PA	PA	PE/PA	PA	PA	PE/PA
SPEC	8	PE/PA	PA	PA	PE/PA	PA	PA	PE/PA	PE/PA
ENGR	8	PE/PA	PA	PA	PE/PA	PE/PA	PA	PA	PE/PA
NOBL	8	PE/PA	PA	PE/PA	PA	PE/PA	PA	PA	PE/PA
BERY	8	PE/PA	PA	PA	PE/PA	PA	PA	PE/PA	PE
COPP	8	PA	PA	PA	PA	PA	PA	PA	PA
SILV	8	NA	NA	NA	NA	NA	NA	NA	NA
GLOR	7	NA	NA	NA	NA	NA	NA	NA	
REIG	4	PE	PE	PE	PE				
CROO	4	PE	PE	PE	PE				
RESI	4	PE	PE	PE	PE				
GREE	4	PE	PE	PE	PE				
ABBE	4	PE	PE	PE	PE				

Image. 1/8. Page 103. Picture showing the photograph of the King and Irene Adler that Sherlock Holmes was asked to locate.
SH-GSF4.

Image. 2/8. Page 105. "il etait taille en hercule et vetu avec une élégance qui touchait au mauvais gout."
("With the chest and limbs of a Hercules. His dress was rich with a richness which would, in England, be looked upon as akin to bad taste.")
SH-GSF5.

Gaston Simoes da Fonseca - Un scandale en Bohême. Premières 1909

Image. 3/8. Page 109. “Un groom a favoris a demi ivre, entra dans la piece.”
(“A drunken-looking groom walked into the room.”)
SH-GSF6.

Image. 4/8. Page 117. “Il me donna tous les renseignements possible sur mademoiselle Adler.”
(“He gave me all the needed information about Miss Adler.”)
SH-GSF7.

Image. 5/8 Page 111. “Je me demandais si je suivrais la voiture a la course.”
(“I was just wondering whether I should not do well to follow them.”)
SH-GSF8.

Image. 6/8. Page 115. “Il poussa un cri et tomba par terre.”
(“He gave a cry and dropped to the ground.”)
SH-GSF9.

Gaston Simoes da Fonseca - Un scandale en Bohême. Premières 1909

Image. 7/8. Page 117. “La dame courut vers la cachette.”
(“She would rush to secure it.”)
SH-GSF10.

Image. 8/8. Page 119. Showing the crown, the King would soon be wearing.
SH-GSF11.

Image 1/8. Page 3. Jabez Wilson copying out from the Encyclopaedia Britannica
SH-GSF12.

Image 2/8. Page 5. “J’ai un petit bueau de prets sur gages.”
(“I have a small pawnbroker's business.”)
SH-GSF13.

Image 3/8. Page 7. “Il cria de toutes ses forces, a la foule, que la place etait prise.”
(“He shouted at the top of his voice that the vacancy was filled.”)
SH-GSF14.

Image 4/8. Page 9. “Il est petit, fort, res vif.”
(“Small, stout-built, very quick in his ways.”)
SH-GSF15.

Image 5/8. Page 12. “Nous engageames dans un couloir sombre.”
(“We went down a dark, earth-smelling passage.”)
SH-GSF16.

Image 6/8. Page 15. “Il se hissa au-dessus du trou.”
(“He stood at the side of the hole.”)
SH-GSF17.

Image 7/8. Page 17. "Sherlock Holmes avai bondi et saisi l'intrus par le cou…"
("Sherlock Holmes had sprung out and seized the intruder by the collar.")
SH-GSF18.

Image 8/8. Page 21. A view of a safe surrounded by 30,000 Gold Napoleons *SH-GSF19.*

Gaston Simoes da Fonseca – Un cas d'identité. Nouvelles 1909

Image. 1/7. Page 23. Mary Sutherland visits Watson and Holmes in Baker Street *SH-GSF20.*

Image. 2/7. Page 25. “Sherlock Holmes la recut avec l’aimable courtoisie qui le caracterait.” (“Sherlock Holmes welcomed her with the easy courtesy for which he was remarkable,”) *SH-GSF21.*

Image. 3/7. Page 27. “Je l’ai rencontre pour la premiere fois au bal.”
(“ ‘I met him first at the gasfitters ball’, she said.”)
SH-GSF22.

Image. 4/7. Page 29. "Je recevais chaque jour une letter de lui."
("He used to write every day.")
SH-GSF23.

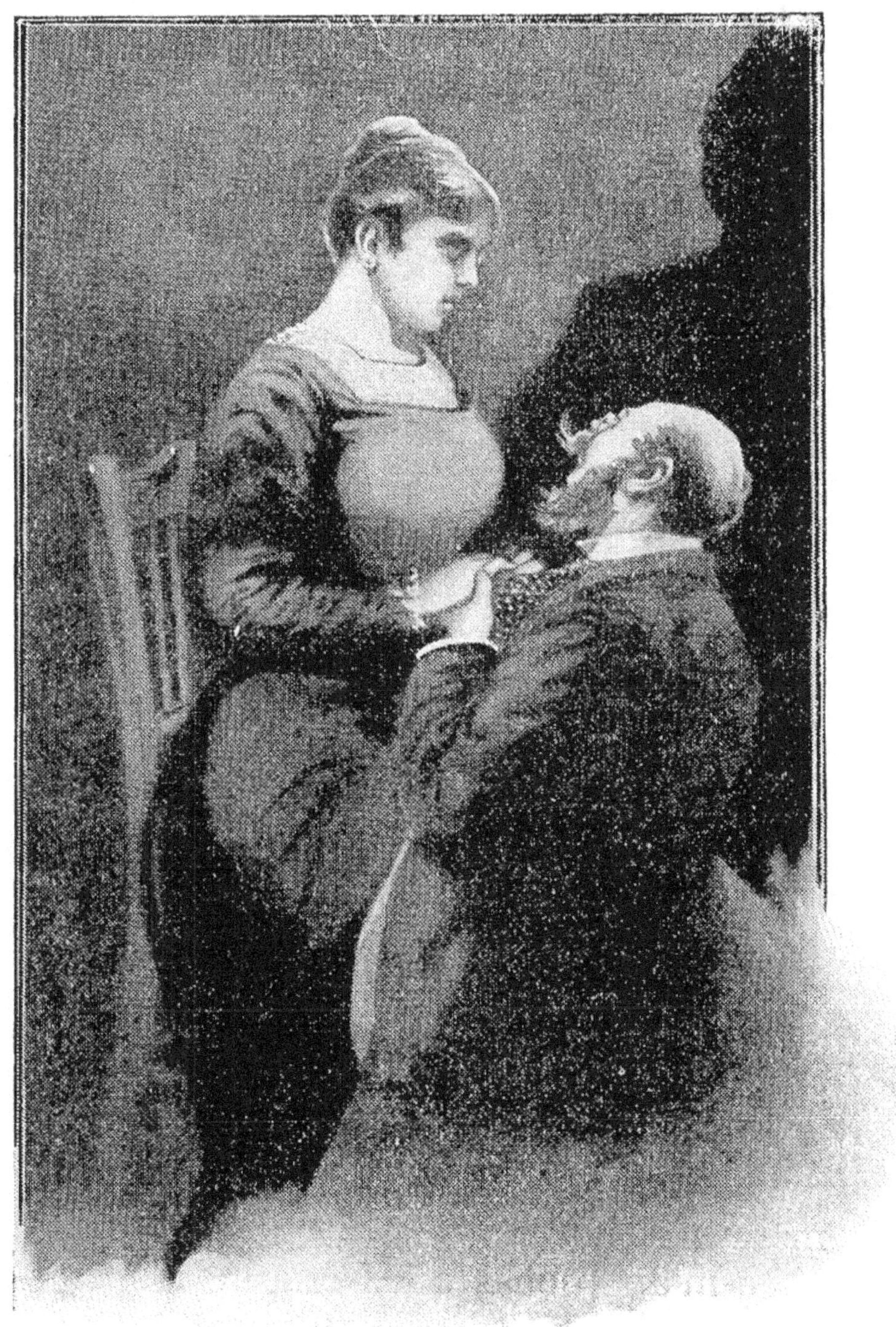

Image. 5/7. Page 31. "Il m'avait fai jurer de lui rester fidele."
("whatever happened, I was to be true;")
SH-GSF24.

Image. 6/7. Page 33. "Elle se retira en promettant de revenir."
("And went her way, with a promise to come again.")
SH-GSF25.

Gaston Simoes da Fonseca – Un cas d'identité. Nouvelles 1909

Image. 7/7. Page 36. The typewriter that helped solve the case.
SH-GSF26.

Image. 1/7. Page 37. Boscombe Valley, the scene of the Crime.
SH-GSF27.

Image. 2/7. Page 39. "M. Mac Carthy et son fils semblaient se disputer violemment."
("Mr. McCarthy and his son, and that they appeared to be having a violent quarrel.")
SH-GSF28.

Image. 3/7. Page 42. "Je m'armat de mon fusil."
("I then took my gun.")
SH-GSF29.

Image. 4/7. Page 45. "J'at vu le jeune mac carthy."
("I have seen young McCarthy.")
SH-GSF30.

Image. 5/7. Page 49. “J’ai peche dedans avec un rateau.”
(“I fished about with a rake.”)
SH-GSF31.

Image. 6/7. Page 51. "Je frappat cet homme avec peu de remords que s'il avait ete une bete mal faisante."
("I struck him down with no more compunction than if he had been some foul and venomous beast.")
SH-GSF32.

Image. 7/7. Page 53. “Black-Jack, de Ballarat”
(“Black Jack of Ballarat.”)
SH-GSF33.

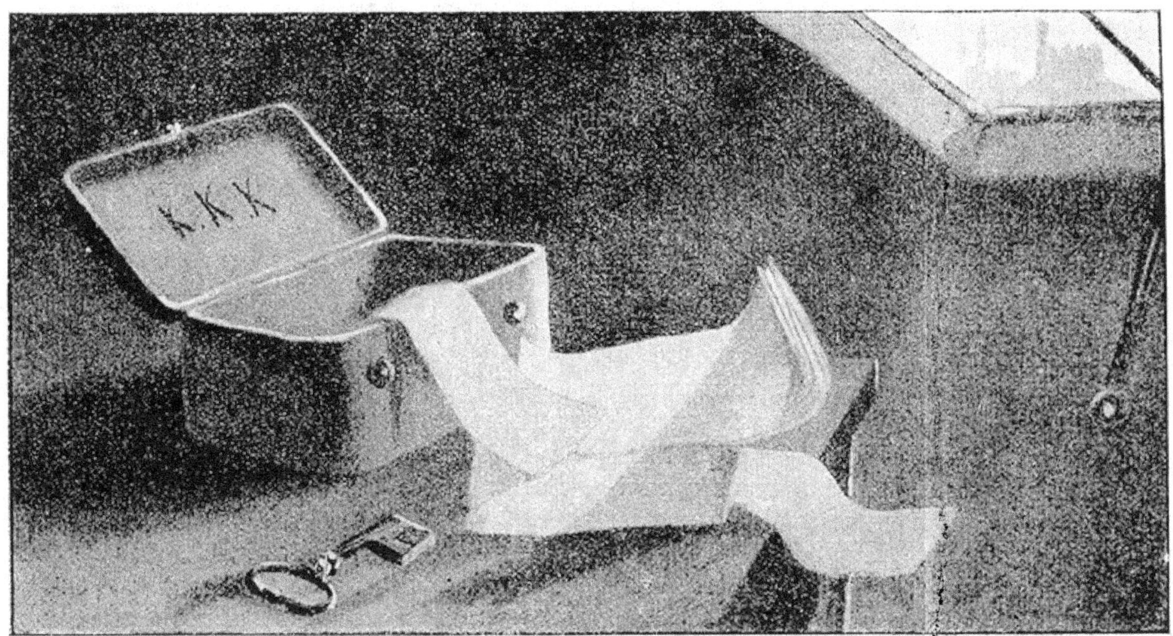

Image. 1/8. Page 57. The mysterious chest that caused so much trouble.
SH-GSF34.

Image. 2/8. Page 59. "J'avais essaye de regarder par le trou de la serrure."
("I have peeped through the keyhole.")
SH-GSF35.

Image. 3/8. Page 61. "Nous le retrouvames la face plongee dans un basin d'eau ccroupie."
("We found him face downwards in a little, green-scummed pool.")
SH-GSF36.

Image. 4/8. Page 63. “Mon pere etait tombe dans une crevasse.”
(“My father had fallen over one of the deep chalk-pits.”)
SH-GSF37.

Image. 5/8. Page 65. “Le vaisseau sur lequel voyageaient ces hommes est un voilier.”
(“The vessel on which these men are travelling is a sailing ship.”)
SH-GSF38.

Image. 6/8. Page 67. "Unpoliceman entendit un appel au secours et un plongeon."
("A Police Constable heard a cry for help and a splash in the water.")
SH-GSF39.

Image. 7/8. Page 69."Je le tiens de la bouche de l’arrimeur."
(“I had it from the stevedore.”)
SH-GSF40.

Image. 8/8. Page 71. Five orange Pips.
SH-GSF41.

Image. 1/7. Page 73.Hugh Boone on the streets.
SH-GSF42.

Image. 2/7. Page 77. “Voyez-vous cette Lumiere a travers les arbres?.”
(“See that light among the trees?”)
SH-GSF43.

Image. 3/7. Page 79. “Il la repoussa dans la rue.”
(“He pushed her out into the street.”)
SH-GSF44.

Image. 4/7. Page 82. “Il se fit une espece de divan oriental.”
(“He constructed a sort of Eastern divan.”)
SH-GSF45.

Image. 5/7. Page 85. “Nous approchames tous deux de la grille.”
(“We both approached the door.”)
SH-GSF46.

Image. 6/7. Page 86. "Je peignis mon visag…"
("I painted my face.")
SH-GSF47.

Image. 7/7. Page 90. Hugh Boone – the man with the twisted lip.
SH-GSF48.

Image 1/8. Page 3. The goose in this story.
SH-GSF49.

Gaston Simoes da Fonseca - L'Escarboucle bleue. Premiers & Premières 1909

Image 2/8. Page 5. " L'homme laisse tomber l'oie, prit ses jambes a son cou et disparut…"
("He dropped his goose, took to his heels, and vanished.")
SH-GSF50.

Image 3/8. Page 8. “James Ryder a temoigne qu’il avait introduit Horner dans le cabinet de toilette de la comiesse.”
(“James Ryder gave his evidence to the effect that he had shown Horner up to the dressing-room of the Countess of Morcar.”)
SH-GSF51.

Image 4/8. Page 11. “La Comtesse a vait l’habitude de mettre ses bijoux dans une petite boite de maroquin.”
(The Countess was accustomed to keep her jewel in a small morocco casket.)
SH-GSF52.

Image 5/8. Page 13. Breckinridge, encadre par la porte, montrait furieusement le poing…"
(Breckinridge, framed in the door of his stall, was shaking his fists fiercely.)
SH-GSF53.

Image 6/8. Page 17. “Ryder se jeta subitement aux genoux d’Holmes.”
(“Ryder clutched at my companion's knees.”)
SH-GSF54.

Image 7/8. Page 16. “Et je sentis la pierre qui descendait dans son jabot.”
(“I felt the stone pass along its gullet.”)
SH-GSF55.

Image 8/8. Page 18. The battered Bowler Hat.
SH-GSF56.

Gaston Simoes da Fonseca - La Bande mouchetée. Premiers & Premières 1909

Image. 1/8. Page 19. Stoke Moran, Home of Helen Stoner, and her Stepfather Grimesby Roylott
SH-GSF57.

Image. 2/8. Page 21. "Il assomma son maître d'hotel indien."
("He beat his native butler to death.")
SH-GSF58.

Image. 3/8. Page 23. “Elle resta en cerain temps a bavarder.”
(“She sat for some time, chatting.”)
SH-GSF59.

Image. 4/8. Page 25. "Elle se tordait comme dans des souffrances horribles."
("She writhed as one who is in terrible pain.")
SH-GSF60.

Image. 5/8. Page 28. "L'apparition d'un homme de forte taille..."
("A huge man framed himself in the aperture...")
SH-GSF61.

Image. 6/8. Page 33. "Sur le coup de onze heures, une vive lumiere perca les tenebres."
("Just at the stroke of eleven, a single bright light shone out.")
SH-GSF62.

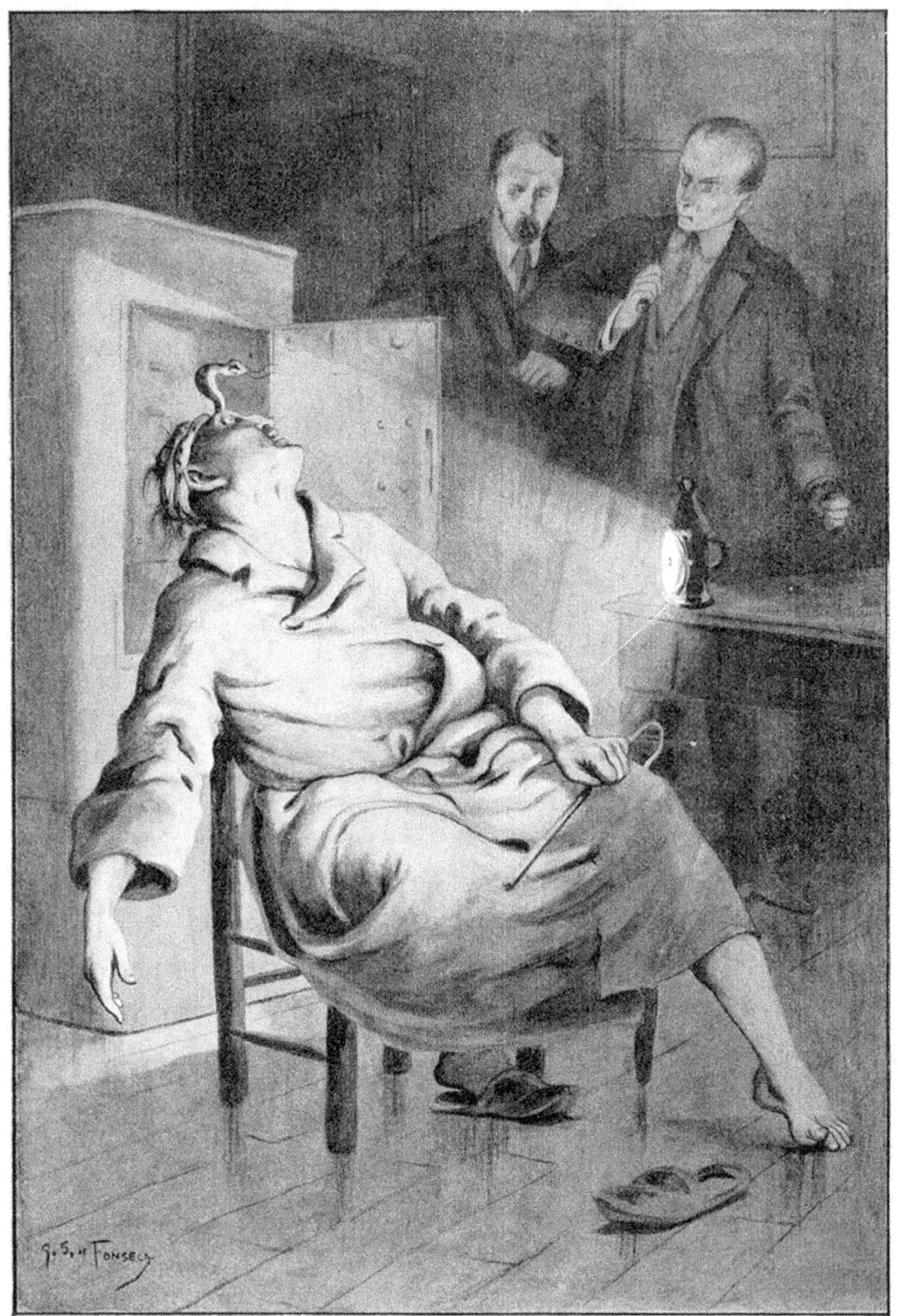

Image. 7/8. Page 293. “Un singulier spectacle s’offrit a nos yeux.”
(“It was a singular sight which met our eyes.”)
SH-GSF63.

Gaston Simoes da Fonseca - La Bande mouchetée. Premiers & Premières 1909

Image. 8/8. Page 36. The Speckled Band – A swamp adder
SH-GSF64.

Image 1/8 Page 37. Fire destroys the home of the Coiners.
SH-GSF65.

Image 2/8. Page 39. J'entrai dans mon cabinet et j'y trouve un homme assis aupres de la table (I entered my consulting-room, and found a gentleman seated by the table.)
SH-GSF66.

Image 3/8. Page 43. Elle perdit toute reserve et fit un pas en a vant, en se ordan les mains. (She threw aside her constraint, and made a step forward, with her hands wrung together.) *SH-GSF67.*

Image 4/8. Page 45. “Hola, Colonel! Ouvrez-moi!”
(“Hallo! Colonel! Let me out!”)
SH-GSF68.

Image 5/8 Page 53. “Fritz me pora un coup de son arme.”
(“Fritz cut at me with his heavy weapon.”)
SH-GSF69.

Image 6/8 Page 49."Je tombai evanoui au milieu des rosiers."
("I fell in a dead faint among the rosebushes.")
SH-GSF70.

Image 7/8 Page 50. “Bradstreet avait etendu une carte militaire du comte sur ses genoux.”
(“Bradstreet had spread an ordnance map of the county out upon the seat.”)
SH-GSF71.

Image 8/8. Page 51. The Coiners making their escape,
SH-GSF72.

Image 1/8 Page 52. The bride makes a quick exit.
SH-GSF73.

Image 2/8 Page 54. "Une femme essaya d'entrer de force dans la maison."
("A woman endeavoured to force her way into the house.")
SH-GSF74.

Gaston Simoes da Fonseca – L'Aristocratique célibataire. Premiers & Premières 1909

Image 3/8 Page 217. “Bonhour, Lord Saint-Simon, dit Holmes, en se levant pour Saluer.”
(“ 'Good day, Lord St Simon,' said Holmes, rising and bowing.”)
SH-GSF75.

Image 4/8 Page 57. "Elle etait habituee a errer seule dans les bois et les montagnes."
("She ran free in a mining camp and wandered through woods or mountains.")
SH-GSF76.

Image 5/8 Page 61. “Un camp de mineurs ataque par les Indiens apaches.”
(“A miners' camp had been attacked by Apache Indians.”)
SH-GSF77.

Image 6/8 Page 63. “Je laissai tomber mon bouquet a l’endroit ou il se trouvait.”
(“I dropped my bouquet over to him.”)
SH-GSF78.

Image 7/8 Page 65. “L’ami Lestrade avait entre les mains des renseignements dont il ignorait la valeur.”
(“Friend Lestrade held information in his hands the value of which he did not himself know.”)
SH-GSF79.

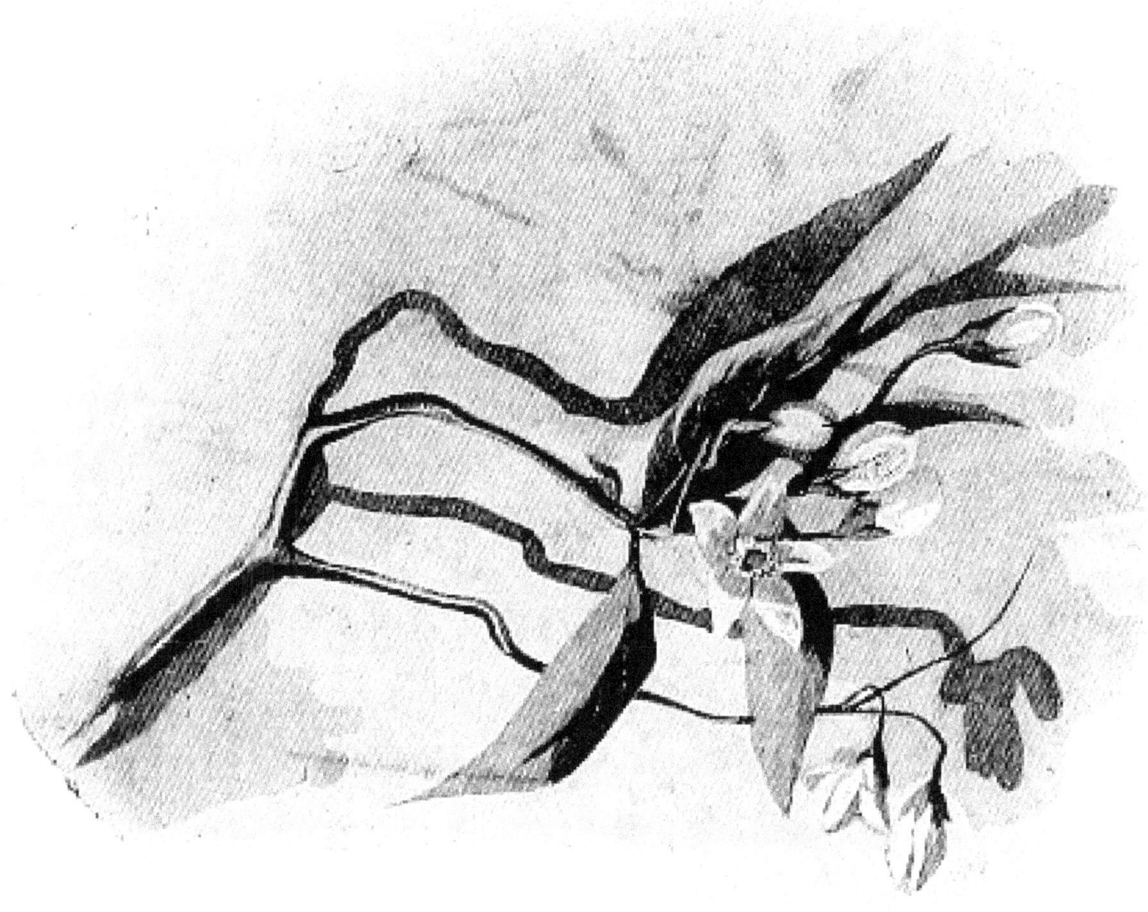

Image 8/8 Page 67. Flowers from the dropped bouquet.
SH-GSF80.

Image 1/8 Page 68. Arthur Holder and Sir George Burnwell fight in the Snow.
SH-GSF81.

Image 2/8 Page 71. “L’homme courait droit a la porte et saisissait la sonnette.”
(“The man rushed at our door and pulled at our bell.”)
SH-GSF82.

Image 3/8 Page 77. “J’apercus Mary a la fenetre de l’antichambre.”
(“I saw Mary herself at the side window of the hall.”)
SH-GSF83.

Image 4/8 Page 75. "J'appelai l'inspecteur, et le lui remis entre les mains."
(" Called in the inspector and gave him into custody.")
SH-GSF84.

Image 5/8 Page 77. "C'est le marchand qui nous apporte des legames, il s'appelle Francis Prosper."
("He is the greengrocer who brings our vegetables round. His name is Francis Prosper.")
SH-GSF85.

Image 6/8 Page 79. “Votre fils etait revenue avec sa prise.”
(“Your son, finding that he had the coronet in his hand.”)
SH-GSF86.

Image 7/8 Page 83. "J'ai vu un vagabond de mauvaise tournure dans la ruelle."
(I saw an ill-dressed vagabond in the lane.)
SH-GSF87.

Gaston Simoes da Fonseca - Le Diadème de béryls. Premières 1909

Image 8/8 Page 123. The Beryl Coronet.
SH-GSF88.

Image. 1/8. Page 85. “Carlo the Mastiff- not a happy ending for him.
SH-GSF89.

Image. 2/8. Page 87. “Oh! Si vous le voyiez tuer des cancrelats avec une pantoufle!”
(“Oh, if you could see him killing cockroaches with a slipper!”)
SH-GSF90.

Image. 3/8. Page 91. “Deux fois, je l’ai vu tout a fait ivre.”
(“Twice since I have seen him quite drunk.”)
SH-GSF91.

Image. 4/8. Page 95. “Mais comment mes propres cheveux pouvalent ils avoir ete enfermes dans ce tiroir?”
(“How could my hair have been locked in the drawer?”)
SH-GSF92.

Image. 5/8. Page 97. “Si vous pouvez la mettre sous clef.”
(“If you can lock it. “)
SH-GSF93.

Image. 6/8. Page 103. “Si jamais vous remettez les pieds ici, je vous donne en pature au matin.”
(“If you ever put your foot over that threshold again, I'll throw you to the mastiff.”)
SH-GSF94.

Image. 7/8. Page 101. "…Et qu'une echelie fut toujours prets pour le moment ou votre maître sortirait."
(". and that a ladder should be ready at the moment when your master had gone out.")
SH-GSF95.

Image. 8/8. Page 102. Carlo's collar now no longer needed.
SH-GSF96.

Image. 1/8. Page 91. The body of John Straker near King's Pyland, Dartmoor
SH-GSF97.

Image. 2/8. Page 94. “Un homme, l’interpellant dans l’obscurite, la pria de s’arreter.” (A man appeared out of the darkness and called to her to stop.)
SH-GSF98.

Image. 3/8. Page 97. “Deux personnes nous attendaient a la gare.”
(Two gentlemen were awaiting us at the station.)
SH-GSF99.

Image. 4/8. Page 101. “Puis, se couchant a plat venre…”
(“Then, lying face down…”)
SH-GSF100.

Image. 5/8. Page 103. "Qu'est-ce que le diable vous amene faire ici?"
("What the devil do you want here?")
SH-GSF101.

Image. 6/8. Page 106. “Il portait les couleurs bien connues…”
(“He wore the well-known colours…”)
SH-GSF102.

Image. 7/8. Page 109. "D'une ruade il fracassa la ete de Straker."
("The steel shoe had struck Straker full on the forehead.")
SH-GSF103.

Gaston Simoes da Fonseca - Silver Blaze Nouvelles. 1909

Image. 8/8. Page 111. Typical kit for horse riding.
SH-GSF104.

Gaston Simoes da Fonseca - Le "Gloria Scott" Nouvelles. 1909

Image. 1/7. Page 113. The Gloria Scott under sail.
SH-GSF105.

Image. 2/7. Page 115. “M. Trevor pere etait un homme riche et considere.”
(“Old Trevor was evidently a man of some wealth and consideration.”)
SH-GSF106.

Image. 3/7. Page 117. “Nous vimes arriver un homme de petite taille, a la tournure vulgaire.”
(“We saw a short man with a vulgar look.”)
SH-GSF107.

Image. 4/7. Page 119. “Une femme de chamber en fleurs vint m’apporter une lampe.”
(“A weeping maid brought in a lamp.”)
SH-GSF108.

Image. 5/7. Page 122. “Derriere lui se tenait l’aumonier, un pistolet encore fumant a la main.”
(“The chaplain stood with a smoking pistol in his hand.”)
SH-GSF109.

Image. 6/7. Page 125. “Assis deviant un baril ouvert, une boite d’allumetes a la main…”
(“with a matchbox in his hand seated beside an open powder barrel.”)
SH-GSF110.

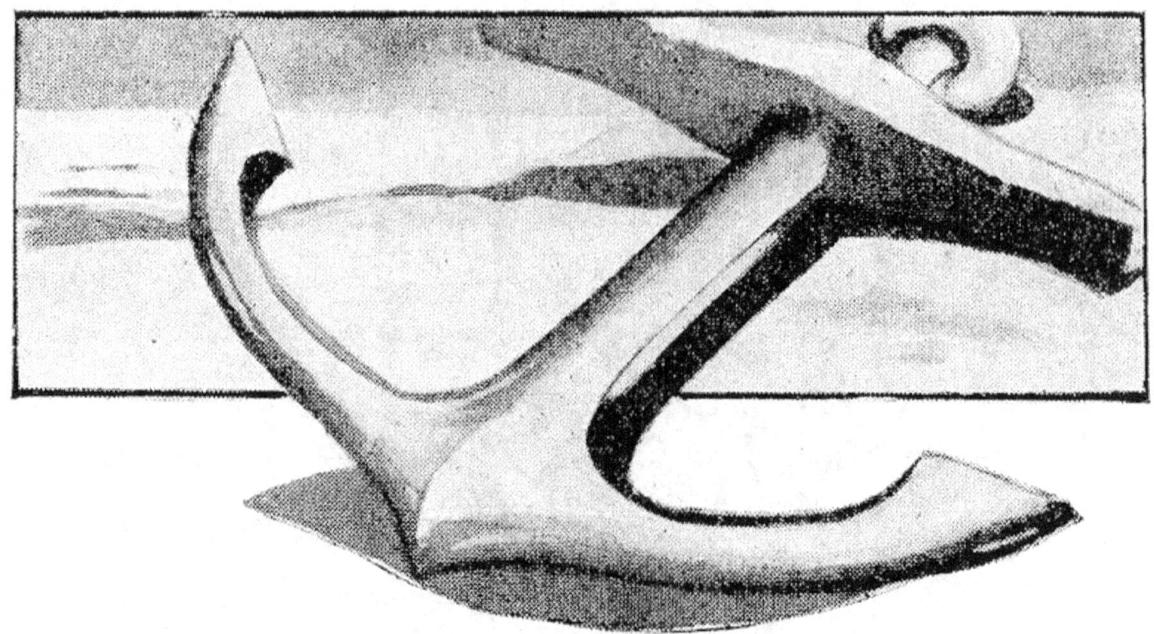

Image. 7/7. Page 126. The anchor of the Gloria Scott? Unlikely.
SH-GSF111.

Image 1/4 Page 5. Poor old Mr. Acton's study after thieves had visited.
SH-GSF112.

Image 2/4 Page 13. “Alec Cunningham aperçut deux hommes lutlant au dehors.”
(“Alec Cunningham saw two men wrestling outside.”)
SH-GSF113.

Image 3/4 Page 24. Les deux Cunningham étaient penchés sur Sherlock Holmes.
(The two Cunninghams were bent over Sherlock Holmes)
SH-GSF114.

Image 4/4 Page 31. The glass smashed into a thousand pieces, and the fruit rolled about into every corner of the room.
SH-GSF115.

Gaston Simoes da Fonseca - The Adventure of the Crooked Man. Premiers 1909

Image 1/4. Page 125. The Crooked man -Henry (Harry) Wood.
SH-GSF116.

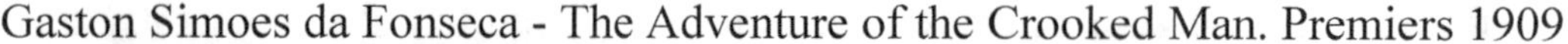

Gaston Simoes da Fonseca - The Adventure of the Crooked Man. Premiers 1909

Image 2/4. Page 133. “Apres trente ans de marriage, elle fai encore sensation.” (“Married for upwards of thirty years, she is still of a striking appearance.”) *SH-GSF117.*

Gaston Simoes da Fonseca - The Adventure of the Crooked Man. Premiers 1909

Image 3/4. Page 141. "Les deux femmes, ainsi que le cocher, resterent dans le vestibule a ecouter la dispute."
("The two women with the coachman came up into the hall and listened to the dispute.")
SH-GSF118.

Image 4/4. Page 148. Teddy The mongoose
SH-GSF119.

Image 1/4. Page 63. The Worthingdon bank gang
SH-GSF120.

Gaston Simoes da Fonseca - Le Malade pensionnaire. Premiers 1909

Image 2/4. Page 72. “Le visieur etai sous le coup de sa mysterieuse maladie.”
(“He was again in the grip of his mysterious malady.”)
SH-GSF121.

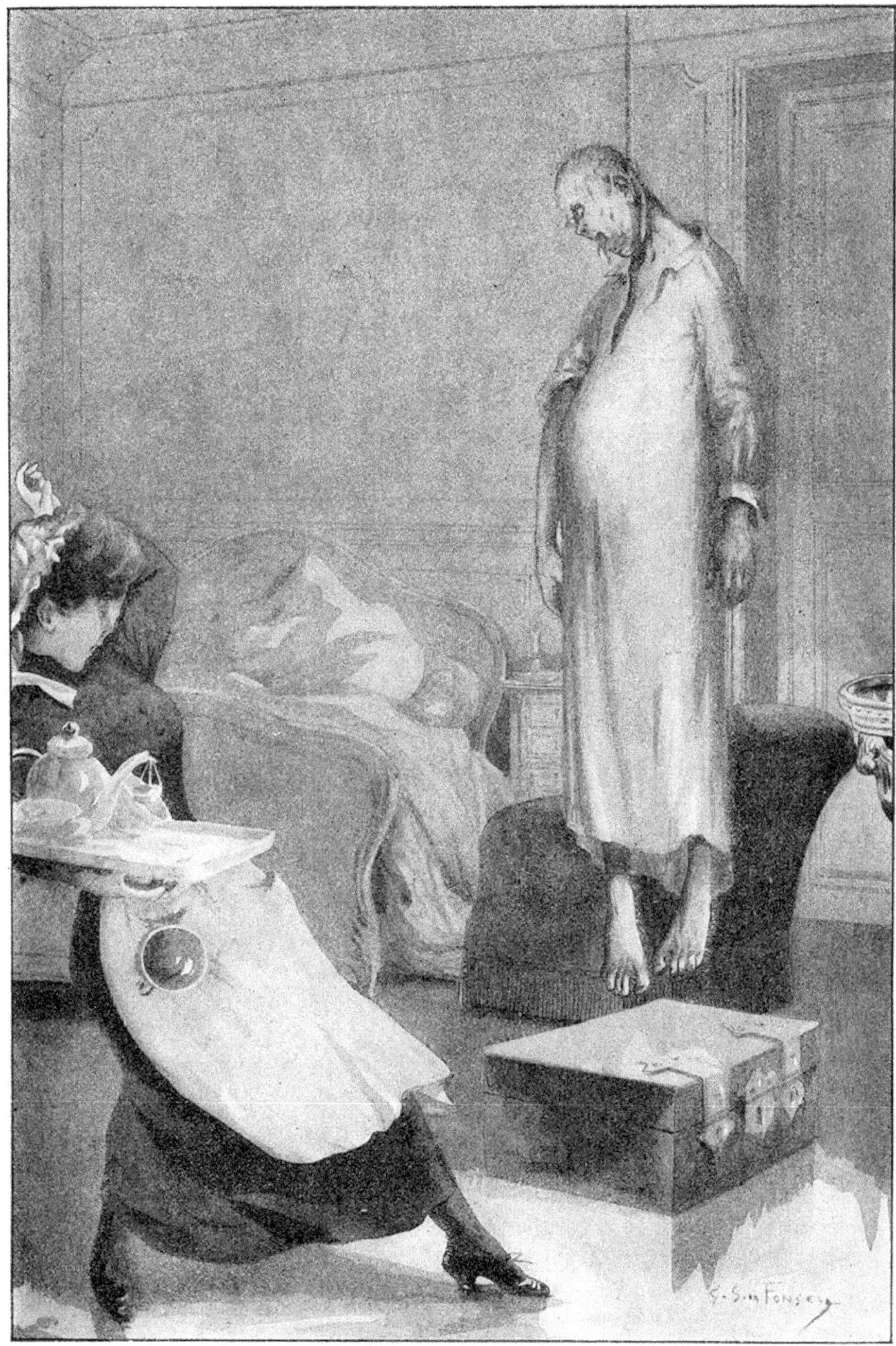

Image 3/4. Page 81. "Elle trouva le malheureux pendu au milieu de la chamber."
("She found the unfortunate fellow hanging in the middle of the room.")
SH-GSF122.

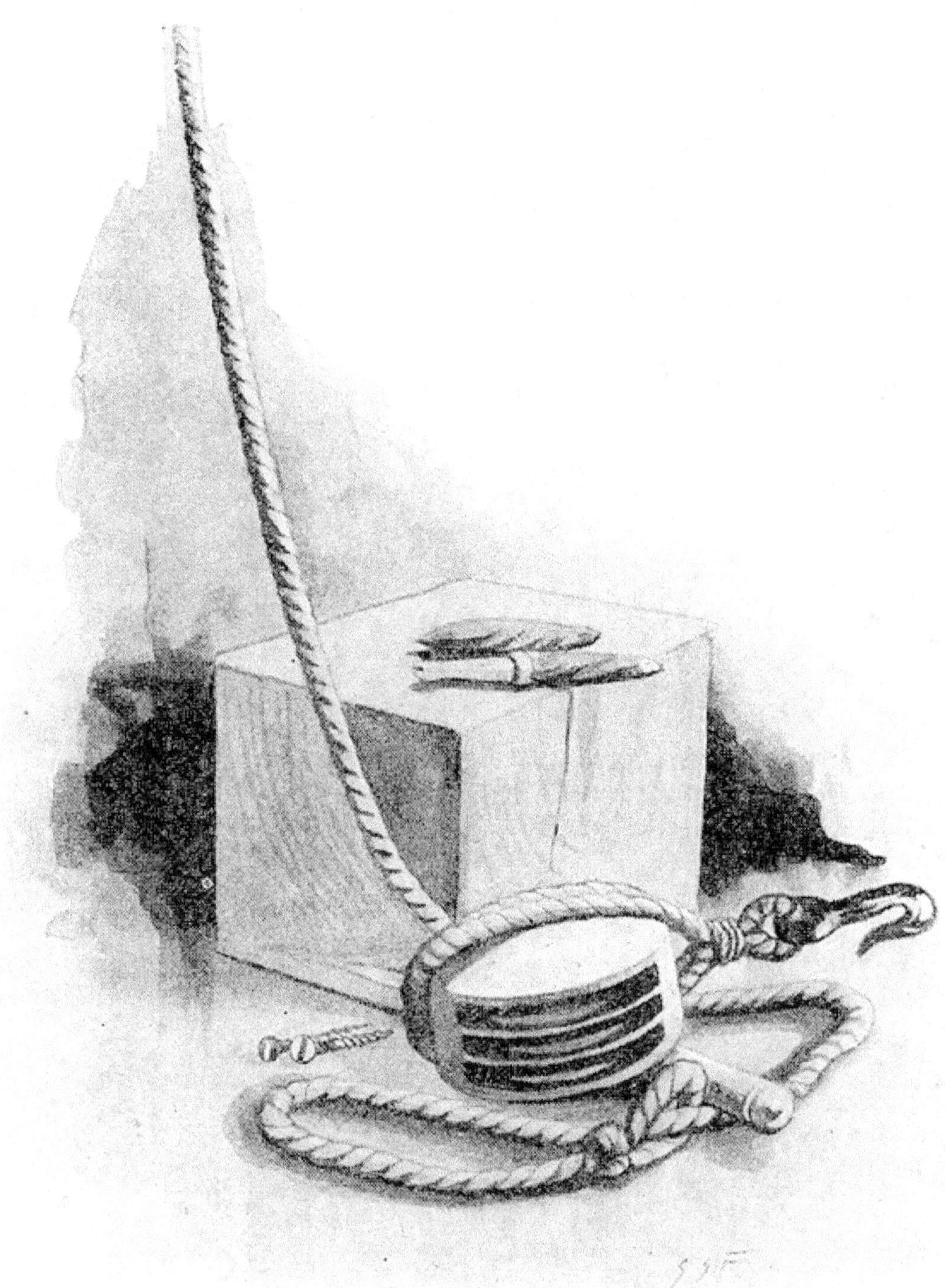

Image 4/4. Page 90. Everything you need to Hang Blessington (Sutton) *SH-GSF123.*

Image 1/4. Page 179. The infamous Carriage.
SH-GSF124.

Image 2/4. Page 189. “C’etait une grande maison sombre, s’elevant pres de la route.” (“A large, dark house, standing back from the road in its own grounds.”) *SH-GSF125.*

Image 3/4. Page 197. “Deux silhouettes appuyees contre le mur.”
(“We saw the vague loom of two figures, which crouched against the wall.”)
SH-GSF126.

Image 4/4. Page 205. 'It's charcoal!' he cried. 'Give it time. It will clear.' *SH-GSF127.*

Image 1/4. Page 237. A Seascape.
SH-GSF128.

Image 2/4. Page 245. “Je m’y suis rendu la nuit derniere et j’ai grate a la fenetre.”
(“I crept round there last night and scratched at the window.”)
SH-GSF129.

Gaston Simoes da Fonseca - L'Abbaye de grange. Premiers. 1909

Image 3/4. Page 257. “A mon tour, je le frappe et lui fracases le crane.”
(“Then it was my turn, and I went through him as if he had been a rotten pumpkin.”)
SH-GSF130.

Gaston Simoes da Fonseca - L'Abbaye de grange. Premiers. 1909

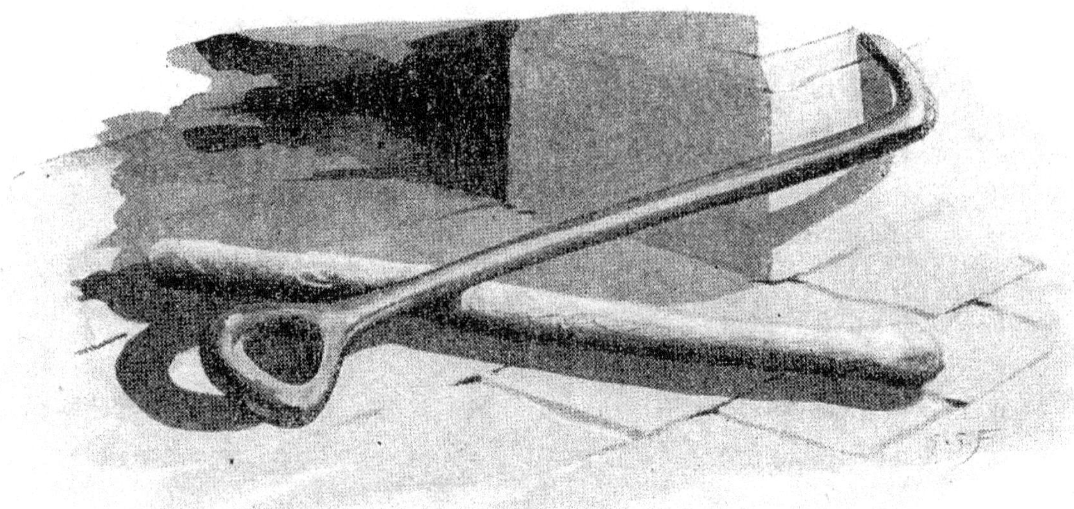

Image 4/4. Page 267. The weapons used in the fight.
SH-GSF131.

Josef Friedrich

Czech name : Josefa Friedricha

Born 1875 in Prague
Died October 1929 in Pilsen

Josef Friedrich was a Czech painter and illustrator who illustrated a number of short stories in three books,

- 'Dobrodružství detektiva Sherlocka Holmesa' (The Adventures of Detective Sherlock Holmes) 1906
- 'Ztracená stopa' (Lost Track) both published by Vilímek in 1906 and
- Mstitel (Avenger) in Prague 1907.

There were a lot of Josefs involved in these Sherlock Holmes books. The stories were translated by Josef Pachmayer, and published by Josef R. Vilímek

He worked in various countries including Germany (Munich) and Argentina (Buenos Aires). He took his inspiration from many Sidney Paget illustrations and when we say inspired, we mean that his images were almost like Paget's taken from another angle. You will find a page reference to Volume 1 Paget images if the image is very similar.

Dobrodružství detektiva Sherlocka Holmesa' 1906

This book contained the 6 stories and 33 images listed below.

Czech Name	Literal Translation	English Name	No. of Images
Skandál v Čechách	A Scandal in The Czech Republic	A Scandal in Bohemia	6
Spolek ryšavců	Association of Red heads	The Red-Headed League	5
Případ totožnosti	Identity Case	A Case of Identity	5
Záhada Boscombského údolí	Mystery Boscombski Valley	The Boscombe Valley Mystery	6
Pět pomerančových jadérek	Five Orange Kernels	The Five Orange Pips	5
Ohyzdný žebrák	Ugly Beggar	The Man with the twisted Lip.	6

Ztracená stopa Prague 1906

Contained 7 stories and 43 images, the first 6 stories were illustrated by Friedrich, but the last story, The Final problem story had Sidney Paget illustrations.

Czech Name	Literal Translation	English Name	No. of Images
Modrá karbunkule	Blue Carbuncle	The Blue Carbuncle	7
Strakatý pás	Spotted Belt	The Speckled Band.	6
Inženýrův palec	Engineer's Thumb	The Engineer's Thumb	6
Urozený ženich	Noble Groom	The Noble Bachelor	5
Berylová korunka	Beryl Crown	The Beryl Coronet	7
Dům U měděných buků	House in Copper Beeches	Copper Beeches	7
Poslední případ	The Last Case	The Final Problem	5 SP

Mstitel 1907 Prague

Was the story Studie v šarlatové (A Study in Scarlet).
Josef Friedrich produced 29 images.

The 100 illustrations and 13 stories will be listed in book, then story order

SCAN, REDH, IDEN, BOSC, FIVE, TWIS, BLUE, SPEC, ENGR, NOBL, BERY, COPP & STUD [1)]

Josef Friedrich – A Scandal in Bohemia, A. 1906 (Dobrodruzství detektiva Sherlocka Holmesa, Vilímek, Prague 1906)

Image 1/6. I saw his tall, spare figure pass twice in a dark silhouette against the blind. *SH-JF1*

Josef Friedrich – A Scandal in Bohemia. 1906. (Dobrodruzství detektiva Sherlocka Holmesa, Vilímek, Prague 1906)

Image 2/6. “Pray take a seat,” said Holmes.
SH-JF2 *see page 34*

Josef Friedrich – A Scandal in Bohemia. 1906 (Dobrodruzství detektiva Sherlocka Holmesa, Vilímek, Prague 1906)

Image 3/6. A drunken-looking groom walked into the room.
SH-JF3

Josef Friedrich – A Scandal in Bohemia. 1906 (Dobrodruzství detektiva Sherlocka Holmesa, Vilímek, Prague 1906)

Image 4/6. "I was half-dragged up to the altar."
SH-JF4

Josef Friedrich – A Scandal in Bohemia. 1906 (Dobrodruzství detektiva Sherlocka Holmesa, Vilímek, Prague 1906)

Image 5/6. He was borne into Briony Lodge.
SH-JF5

Josef Friedrich – A Scandal in Bohemia. 1906 (Dobrodruzství detektiva Sherlocka Holmesa, Vilímek, Prague 1906)

Image 6/6. "This photograph!"
SH-JF6

Josef Friedrich – The Red-Headed League. 1906. (Dobrodruzství detektiva Sherlocka Holmesa, Vilímek, Prague 1906)

Image 1/5. "Here it is. This is what began it all."
SH-JF7 *see page 42.*

Josef Friedrich – The Red-Headed League. 1906 (Dobrodruzství detektiva Sherlocka Holmesa, Vilímek, Prague 1906)

Image 2/5. "Here's another vacancy on the league of the red-headed men."

SH-JF8 *see page 43.*

Josef Friedrich – The Red-Headed League. 1906 (Dobrodruzství detektiva Sherlocka Holmesa, Vilímek, Prague 1906)

Image 3/5. The door was instantly opened by a fellow, who asked him to step in.
SH-JF9 *see page 47*

Josef Friedrich – The Red-Headed League. 1906 (Dobrodruzství detektiva Sherlocka Holmesa, Vilímek, Prague 1906)

Image 4/5. Mr. Merryweather stopped to light a lantern.
SH-JF10 *see page 49*

Josef Friedrich – The Red-Headed League. 1906 (Dobrodruzství detektiva Sherlocka Holmesa, Vilímek, Prague 1906)

Image 5/5. "It's no use, John Clay."
SH-JF11 *see page 50.*

Josef Friedrich – A Case of Identity. 1906. (Dobrodruzství detektiva Sherlocka Holmesa, Vilímek, Prague 1906)

Image 1/5. “I am not convinced of it,” I answered.
SH-JF12

Josef Friedrich – A Case of Identity. 1906. (Dobrodruzství detektiva Sherlocka Holmesa, Vilímek, Prague 1906)

Image 2/5. Sherlock Holmes welcomed her.
SH-JF13 *see page 51*

Josef Friedrich – A Case of Identity. 1906. (Dobrodruzství detektiva Sherlocka Holmesa, Vilímek, Prague 1906)

Image 3/5. "There was no one there!"
SH-JF14 *see page 53*

Josef Friedrich – A Case of Identity. 1906. (Dobrodruzství detektiva Sherlocka Holmesa, Vilímek, Prague 1906)

Image 4/5. "Certainly," said Holmes, stepping over and turning the key in the door. *SH-JF15*

Josef Friedrich – A Case of Identity. 1906. (Dobrodruzství detektiva Sherlocka Holmesa, Vilímek, Prague 1906)

Image 5/5. Before he could grasp it there was a wild clatter of steps upon the stairs.
SH-JF16 *see page 57*

Josef Friedrich – The Boscombe Valley Mystery. 1906. (Dobrodruzství detektiva Sherlocka Holmesa, Vilímek, Prague 1906)

Image 1/6. "On following him they found the dead body stretched out upon the grass beside the pool.".

SH-JF17 *see page 59*

Josef Friedrich – The Boscombe Valley Mystery. 1906. (Dobrodruzství detektiva Sherlocka Holmesa, Vilímek, Prague 1906)

Image 2/6. “Oh, Mr. Sherlock Holmes!” she cried.
SH-JF18

Josef Friedrich – The Boscombe Valley Mystery. 1906. (Dobrodruzství detektiva Sherlocka Holmesa, Vilímek, Prague 1906)

Image 3/6. I lay upon the sofa and tried to interest myself in a yellow-backed novel.
SH-JF19

Josef Friedrich – The Boscombe Valley Mystery. 1906. (Dobrodruzství detektiva Sherlocka Holmesa, Vilímek, Prague 1906)

Image 4/6. Swiftly and silently, he made his way along the track.
SH-JF20

Josef Friedrich – The Boscombe Valley Mystery. 1906. (Dobrodruzství detektiva Sherlocka Holmesa, Vilímek, Prague 1906)

Image 5/6. The man who entered was a strange and impressive figure.
SH-JF21 *see page 66*

Josef Friedrich – The Boscombe Valley Mystery. 1906. (Dobrodruzství detektiva Sherlocka Holmesa, Vilímek, Prague 1906)

Image 6/6. "I smoked a cigar and waited behind a tree."
SH-JF22 *see page 65*

Josef Friedrich – The Five Orange Pips. 1906. (Dobrodruzství detektiva Sherlocka Holmesa, Vilímek, Prague 1906)

Image 1/5. The man who entered was young.
SH-JF23 *see page 68*

Josef Friedrich – The Five Orange Pips. 1906. (Dobrodruzství detektiva Sherlocka Holmesa, Vilímek, Prague 1906)

Image 2/5. "We found him, when we went to search for him."
SH-JF24

Josef Friedrich – The Five Orange Pips. 1906. (Dobrodruzství detektiva Sherlocka Holmesa, Vilímek, Prague 1906)

Image 3/5. "There he was, sitting with a newly opened envelope."
SH-JF25

Josef Friedrich – The Five Orange Pips. 1906. (Dobrodruzství detektiva Sherlocka Holmesa, Vilímek, Prague 1906)

Image 4/5. He lit his pipe and leaning back in his chair he watched the blue smoke-rings. *SH-JF26*

Josef Friedrich – The Five Orange Pips. 1906. (Dobrodruzství detektiva Sherlocka Holmesa, Vilímek, Prague 1906)

Image 5/5. That hurts my pride, Watson' he said.
SH-JF27

Josef Friedrich – The Man with the Twisted Lip. 1906. (Dobrodruzství detektiva Sherlocka Holmesa, Vilímek, Prague 1906)

Image 1/6. There sat a tall, thin old man, staring into the fire.
SH-JF28

Josef Friedrich – The Man with the Twisted Lip. 1906. (Dobrodruzství detektiva Sherlocka Holmesa, Vilímek, Prague 1906)

Image 2/6. He flicked the horse with his whip.
SH-JF29

Josef Friedrich – The Man with the Twisted Lip. 1906. (Dobrodruzství detektiva Sherlocka Holmesa, Vilímek, Prague 1906)

Image 3/6. Mrs. St. Clair had fainted at the sight of the blood.
SH-JF30 *see page 79*

Josef Friedrich – The Man with the Twisted Lip. 1906. (Dobrodruzství detektiva Sherlocka Holmesa, Vilímek, Prague 1906)

Image 4/6. Sherlock Holmes sprang out of his chair as if he had been galvanized. *SH-JF31*

Josef Friedrich – The Man with the Twisted Lip. 1906. (Dobrodruzství detektiva Sherlocka Holmesa, Vilímek, Prague 1906)

Image 5/6. So, he sat as I dropped off to sleep.
SH-JF32 *see page 81*

Josef Friedrich – The Man with the Twisted Lip. 1906. (Dobrodruzství detektiva Sherlocka Holmesa, Vilímek, Prague 1906)

Image 6/6. There, sitting up in his bed, was a pale, sad-faced, refined-looking man. *SH-JF33*

Josef Friedrich – The Blue Carbuncle. 1906. (Ztracená stopa, Vilímek, Prague 1906)

Image 1/7. He was left in possession of the field of battle.
SH-JF34 *see page 85*

Josef Friedrich – The Blue Carbuncle. 1906.
(Ztracená stopa, Vilímek, Prague 1906)

Image 2/7. "See here, Sir! See what my wife found in its crop!"
SH-JF35 *see page 86*

Josef Friedrich – The Blue Carbuncle. 1906.
(Ztracená stopa, Vilímek, Prague 1906)

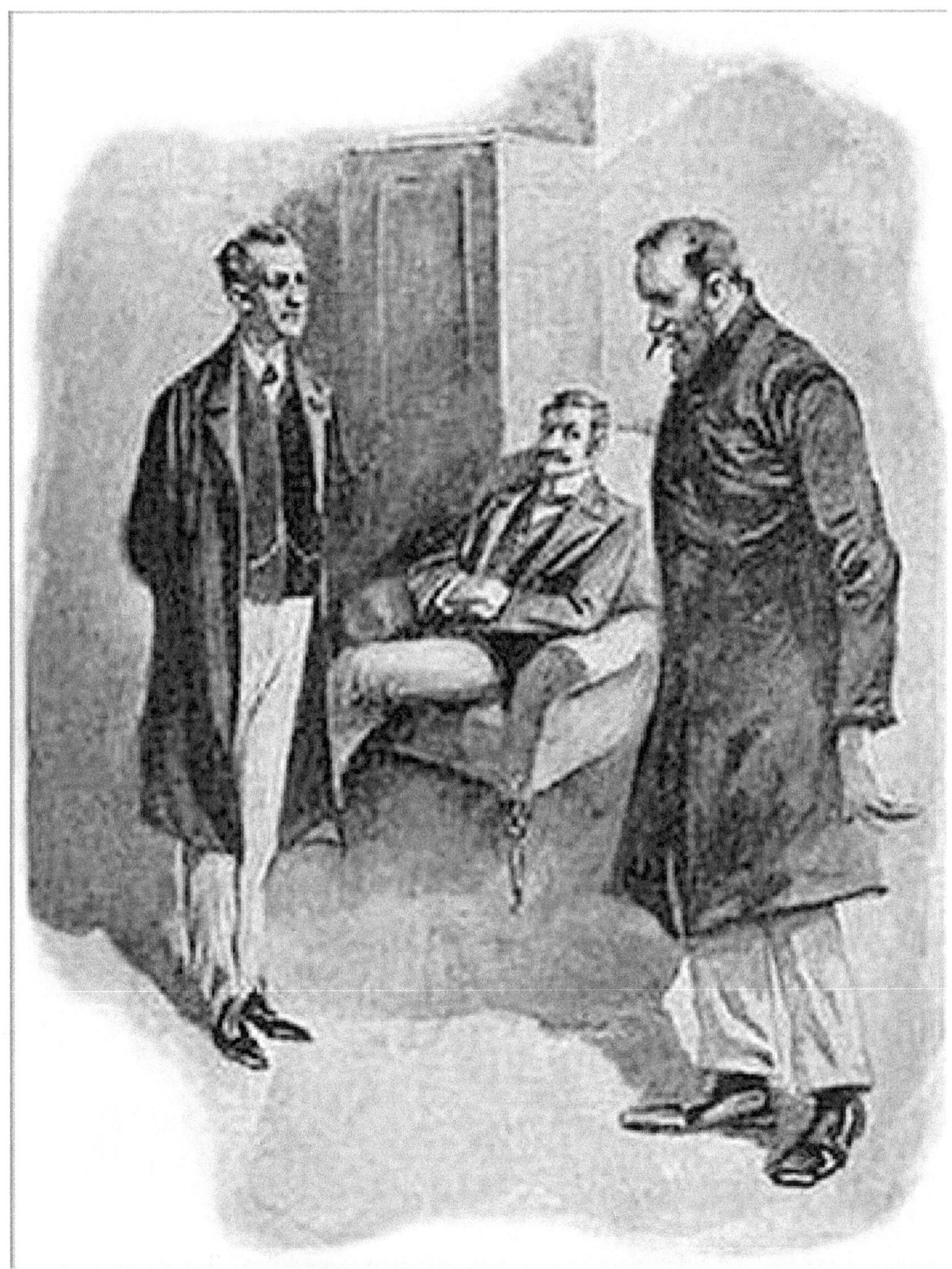

Image 3/7. “Mr. Henry Baker, I believe,” said he.
SH-JF36

Josef Friedrich – The Blue Carbuncle. 1906.
(Ztracená stopa, Vilímek, Prague 1906)

Image 4/7. The salesman nodded and shot a questioning glance at my companion.
SH-JF37 *see page 88*

Josef Friedrich – The Blue Carbuncle. 1906.
(Ztracená stopa, Vilímek, Prague 1906)

Image 5/7. "Oh, Sir, you are the very man whom I have longed to meet," cried the little fellow.
SH-JF38 *see page 89*

Josef Friedrich – The Blue Carbuncle. 1906.
(Ztracená stopa, Vilímek, Prague 1906)

Image 6/7. What a shrimp it is, to be sure!
SH-JF39 *see page 90*

Josef Friedrich – The Blue Carbuncle. 1906.
(Ztracená stopa, Vilímek, Prague 1906)

Image 7/7. He burst into convulsive sobbing, with his face buried in his hands.
SH-JF40 *see page 91*

Josef Friedrich – The Speckled Band. 1906.
(Ztracená stopa, Vilímek, Prague 1906)

Image 1/6. The Lady gave a violent start and stared in bewilderment at my companion.
SH-JF41

Josef Friedrich – The Speckled Band. 1906.
(Ztracená stopa, Vilímek, Prague 1906)

Image 2/6. She writhed as one who is in terrible pain, and her limbs were dreadfully convulsed.
SH-JF42

Josef Friedrich – The Speckled Band. 1906.
(Ztracená stopa, Vilímek, Prague 1906)

Image 3/6. A huge man framed himself in the aperture.
SH-JF43 *see page 95*

Josef Friedrich – The Speckled Band. 1906.
(Ztracená stopa, Vilímek, Prague 1906)

Image 4/6. some scaffolding had been erected against the end wall.
SH-JF44

Josef Friedrich – The Speckled Band. 1906.
(Ztracená stopa, Vilímek, Prague 1906)

Image 5/6. "My God!" I whispered, "Did you see it?"
SH-JF45

Josef Friedrich – The Speckled Band. 1906.
(Ztracená stopa, Vilímek, Prague 1906)

Image 6/6. some scaffolding had been erected against the end wall.
SH-JF46 *see page 100*

Josef Friedrich – The Engineer's Thumb. 1906.
(Ztracená stopa, Vilímek, Prague 1906)

Image 1/6. I took it up and glanced at it.
SH-JF47

Josef Friedrich – The Engineer's Thumb. 1906.
(Ztracená stopa, Vilímek, Prague 1906)

Image 2/6. "I shall start at once upon my peculiar experiences."
SH-JF48

Josef Friedrich – The Engineer's Thumb. 1906.
(Ztracená stopa, Vilímek, Prague 1906)

Image 3/6. "Absolute and complete silence, before, during, and after?"
SH-JF49 *see page 104*

Josef Friedrich – The Engineer's Thumb. 1906.
(Ztracená stopa, Vilímek, Prague 1906)

Image 4/6. "For the love of Heaven!" she whispered, "Get away from here before it is too late!"
SH-JF50 *see page 105*

Josef Friedrich – The Engineer's Thumb. 1906.
(Ztracená stopa, Vilímek, Prague 1906)

Image 5/6. "I threw myself, screaming, against the door, and dragged with my nails at the lock."
SH-JF51 *see page 106*

Josef Friedrich – The Engineer's Thumb. 1906.
(Ztracená stopa, Vilímek, Prague 1906)

Image 6/6. "He has seen too much. Let me pass, I say!"
SH-JF52

Josef Friedrich – The Noble Bachelor. 1906.
(Ztracená stopa, Vilímek, Prague 1906)

Image 1/5. "Here he is," said he, sitting down and flattening it out upon his knee.
SH-JF53

Josef Friedrich – The Noble Bachelor. 1906.
(Ztracená stopa, Vilímek, Prague 1906)

Image 2/5. She was ejected by the butler and the footman.
SH-JF54 *see page 110*

Josef Friedrich – The Noble Bachelor. 1906.
(Ztracená stopa, Vilímek, Prague 1906)

Image 3/5. The gentleman in the pew handed it up to her again.
SH-JF55 *see page 112*

Josef Friedrich – The Noble Bachelor. 1906.
(Ztracená stopa, Vilímek, Prague 1906)

Image 4/5. He took up the paper in a listless way, but his attention instantly riveted. *SH-JF56*

Josef Friedrich – The Noble Bachelor. 1906.
(Ztracená stopa, Vilímek, Prague 1906)

Image 5/5. "Then you won't forgive me? You won't shake hands before I go?"
SH-JF57

Josef Friedrich – The Beryl Coronet. 1906.
(Ztracená stopa, Vilímek, Prague 1906)

Image 1/7. The man sat for a minute or more with a heaving chest.
SH-JF58

Josef Friedrich – The Beryl Coronet. 1906
(Ztracená stopa, Vilímek, Prague 1906)

Image 2/7. I unlocked my bureau, made sure that my treasure was safe."
SH-JF59 *see page 118*

Josef Friedrich – The Beryl Coronet. 1906
(Ztracená stopa, Vilímek, Prague 1906)

Image 3/7. "At my cry he dropped it from his grasp and turned as pale as death."
SH-JF60 *see page 120*

Josef Friedrich – The Beryl Coronet. 1906
(Ztracená stopa, Vilímek, Prague 1906)

Image 4/7. She went straight to her uncle.
SH-JF61

Josef Friedrich – The Beryl Coronet. 1906
(Ztracená stopa, Vilímek, Prague 1906)

Image 5/7. He was down again in a few minutes dressed as a common loafer.
SH-JF62

Josef Friedrich – The Beryl Coronet. 1906
(Ztracená stopa, Vilímek, Prague 1906)

Image 6/7. "In the scuffle, your son struck Sir George, and cut him over the eye."
SH-JF63 *see page 124*

Josef Friedrich – The Beryl Coronet. 1906
(Ztracená stopa, Vilímek, Prague 1906)

Image 7/7. "I clapped a pistol to his head before he could strike."
SH-JF64 *see page 125*

Josef Friedrich – The Copper Beeches. 1906.
(Ztracená stopa, Vilímek, Prague 1906)

Image 1/7. The door opened, and a young Lady entered the room.
SH-JF65

Josef Friedrich – The Copper Beeches. 1906.
(Ztracená stopa, Vilímek, Prague 1906)

Image 2/7. "You are looking for a situation, Miss?" he asked.
SH-JF66 *see page 127*

Josef Friedrich – The Copper Beeches. 1906.
(Ztracená stopa, Vilímek, Prague 1906)

Image 3/7. "They always fill me with a certain horror."
SH-JF67

Josef Friedrich – The Copper Beeches. 1906.
(Ztracená stopa, Vilímek, Prague 1906)

Image 4/7. "I read for about ten minutes."
SH-JF68 *see page 130*

Josef Friedrich – The Copper Beeches. 1906.
(Ztracená stopa, Vilímek, Prague 1906)

Image 5/7. "I laid the two tresses together."
SH-JF69 *see page 131*

Josef Friedrich – The Copper Beeches. 1906.
(Ztracená stopa, Vilímek, Prague 1906)

Image 6/7. "What has frightened you, my dear young Lady?"
SH-JF70

Josef Friedrich – The Copper Beeches. 1906.
(Ztracená stopa, Vilímek, Prague 1906)

Image 7/7. Running up, I blew it's brains out.
SH-JF71 *see page 134*

Josef Friedrich – A Study in Scarlet.
(Mstitel, Vilímek, Prague 1907)

Viděl k svému úžasu muže, ležícího na zemi . . .

Image 1/29. Used on Book cover, Frontispiece & Page.185.
Vidčl k svému úžasu muže, ležiciho na zemi ….
(To his amazement, he saw a man lying on the ground…)
SH-JF72

Josef Friedrich – A Study in Scarlet
(Mstitel, Vilímek, Prague 1907)

Byl jsem raněn na rameni kulí . . . (Str. 8.)

Image 2/29. Page 9.
byl jsem raněn na rameni kuli ... (Str. 8)
(I was wounded on the shoulder by a bullet ... p. 8)
SH-JF73

Josef Friedrich – A Study in Scarlet
(Mstitel, Vilímek, Prague 1907)

„Byl jste v Afganistanu, jak vidím," pravil Holmes . . . (Str. 16.)

Image 3/29. Page 17.
"Byl jste v afganistanu, jak vidim," pravil Holmes... (Str. 16)
("You were in Afghanistan, I see," Holmes said... p. 16)
SH-JF74

Josef Friedrich – A Study in Scarlet
(Mstitel, Vilímek, Prague 1907)

Image 4/29. Page 25. "... pohrával smyčcem na zdař bůh po strunách ... (Str. 31)
(... played the bow on the strings with good luck ... p. 31)
SH-JF75

Josef Friedrich – A Study in Scarlet
(Mstitel, Vilímek, Prague 1907)

„Jaký to nevýslovný žvast!“ zvolal jsem . . . (Str. 35.)

Image 5/29. Page 41.
"Jaký nevýslovný žvast!" zvolal jsem... (Str. 35)
("What an unspeakable news!" I called ... p. 35)
SH-JF76

Josef Friedrich – A Study in Scarlet
(Mstitel, Vilímek, Prague 1907)

„Pro pana Sherlocka Holmesa," pravil . . . (Str. 42)

Image 6/29. Page 53.
"Pro pana Sherlocka Holmesa," pravil... (Str.42)
("For Mr. Sherlock Holmes," he said ... p.42)
SH-JF77

Josef Friedrich – A Study in Scarlet
(Mstitel, Vilímek, Prague 1907)

„Tento případ způsobí hodně hluku, pane" . . . (Str. 55.)

Image 7/29. Page 61.
"Tenro případ způsobi hodně hluku, pane".... (Str.55)
("This case will make a lot of noise, sir" ....p.55)
SH-JF78

Josef Friedrich – A Study in Scarlet
(Mstitel, Vilímek, Prague 1907)

Rozžehl sirku o svoji botu a přidržel ji ke stěně . . . (Str. 60.)

Image 8/29. Page 69.
Rozžehl sirku o svoji botu a přidržel ji ke stěně.... (Str.60)
(He lit a match on his shoe and held it against the wall ....p.60)
SH-JF79

Josef Friedrich – A Study in Scarlet
(Mstitel, Vilímek, Prague 1907)

Audleyův dvůr nebyl vábivým místem . . . (Str. 72.)

Image 9/29. Page 73.
Audleyův dvůr nebyl lákavým místem... (str. 72.)
(Audley's court was not a tempting place ... p. 72.)
SH-JF80

Josef Friedrich – A Study in Scarlet
(Mstitel, Vilímek, Prague 1907)

Image 10/29. Page 89.
Rance vyskočil s tváří.vytíeštěno ... (Str. 76)
Rance jumped up with his face printed ... (p. 76)
SH-JF81

Josef Friedrich – A Study in Scarlet
(Mstitel, Vilímek, Prague 1907)

Uklonivši se znova, pravila . . . (Str. 88.)

Image 11/29. Page 97.
Uklonivši se znova, pravila... (Str.88)
She bowed again ... (P.88)
SH-JF82

Josef Friedrich – A Study in Scarlet
(Mstitel, Vilímek, Prague 1907)

„Pozor!“ zvolal Holmes ostrým tónem . . . (Str. 100.)

Image 12/29. Page 109.
"Pozor!" zvolal Holmes Ostrým tónem... (Str. 100)
("Attention!" exclaimed Holmes Sharp tone ... p. 100)
SH-JF83

Josef Friedrich – A Study in Scarlet
(Mstitel, Vilímek, Prague 1907)

. . chytil ji za ruku a snažil se táhnouti ji ke dveřím . . . (Str. 108.)

Image 13/29. Page 117.
…chytil ji za ruku a snažil se táhnouti ji ke dveřim... (Str. 108)
(… He grabbed her hand and tried to pull her to the door p. 108)
SH-JF84

Josef Friedrich – A Study in Scarlet
(Mstitel, Vilímek, Prague 1907)

. Gregson vyskočil se své stolice . . . (Str. 113)

Image 14/29. Page 121.
Gregson vyskočil se své stolice... (Str. 113)
(Gregson jumped out of his chair ... p. 113)
SH-JF85

Josef Friedrich – A Study in Scarlet
(Mstitel, Vilímek, Prague 1907)

Pes ležel dále natažen na podušce . . . (Str. 122.)

Image 15/29. Page 129.
Pes ležel dále natažen na podušce... (Str. 122)
(The dog was still lying on the pillow ... p. 122)
SH-JF86

Josef Friedrich – A Study in Scarlet
(Mstitel, Vilímek, Prague 1907)

. . . nyní počal trašlivý zápas . . (Str. 130.)

Image 16/29. Page 141.
…nyni počal trašlivý zápas (Str. 130.)
(Now started a terrible wrestle… p. 130.)
SH-JF87

Josef Friedrich – A Study in Scarlet
(Mstitel, Vilímek, Prague 1907)

Těsně podle sebe na úzkém shawlu klečeli dva poutnici . . (Str. 142.)

Image 17/29. Page 149.
Těsně podle sebe na úzkém shawlu klečeli dva poutnici..(Str. 142)
(Two pilgrims were kneeling close to each other on a narrow shawl ... p. 142)
SH-JF88

Josef Friedrich – A Study in Scarlet
(Mstitel, Vilímek, Prague 1907)

Jeden z mužů zvedl malou dívku na svá ramena . . . (Str. 148.)

Image 18/29. Page 157.
Jeden z mužů zvedl malou divku na svá ramana... (Str. 148)
(One of the men raised the little girl onto his shoulder ... p. 148)
SH-JF89

Josef Friedrich – A Study in Scarlet
(Mstitel, Vilímek, Prague 1907)

Malá Lucie byla vezena dost příjemně . . . (Str. 155.)

Image 19/29. Page 161.
Malá Lucie byla vezena dost přijemné... (Str. 155)
(Little Lucy was imprisoned enough ... (p. 155))
SH-JF90

Josef Friedrich – A Study in Scarlet
(Mstitel, Vilímek, Prague 1907)

. . . pevná, snědá ruka zachytla koně za uzdu . . . (Str. 162.)

Image 20/29. Page 169.
…pevná, snědá ruka zachytla koně za uzdu... (str. 162.)
(... a firm, brown hand caught the horse by the bridle ... p. 162)
SH-JF91

Josef Friedrich – A Study in Scarlet
(Mstitel, Vilímek, Prague 1907)

„Bratře Ferriere," pravil, usedaje . . (Str. 173.)

Image 21/29. Page 181.
"Bratře Ferriere," pravil, usedaje… (str. 173)
("Brother Ferriere," he said, sitting down … (p. 173)
SH-JF92

Josef Friedrich – A Study in Scarlet
(Mstitel, Vilímek, Prague 1907)

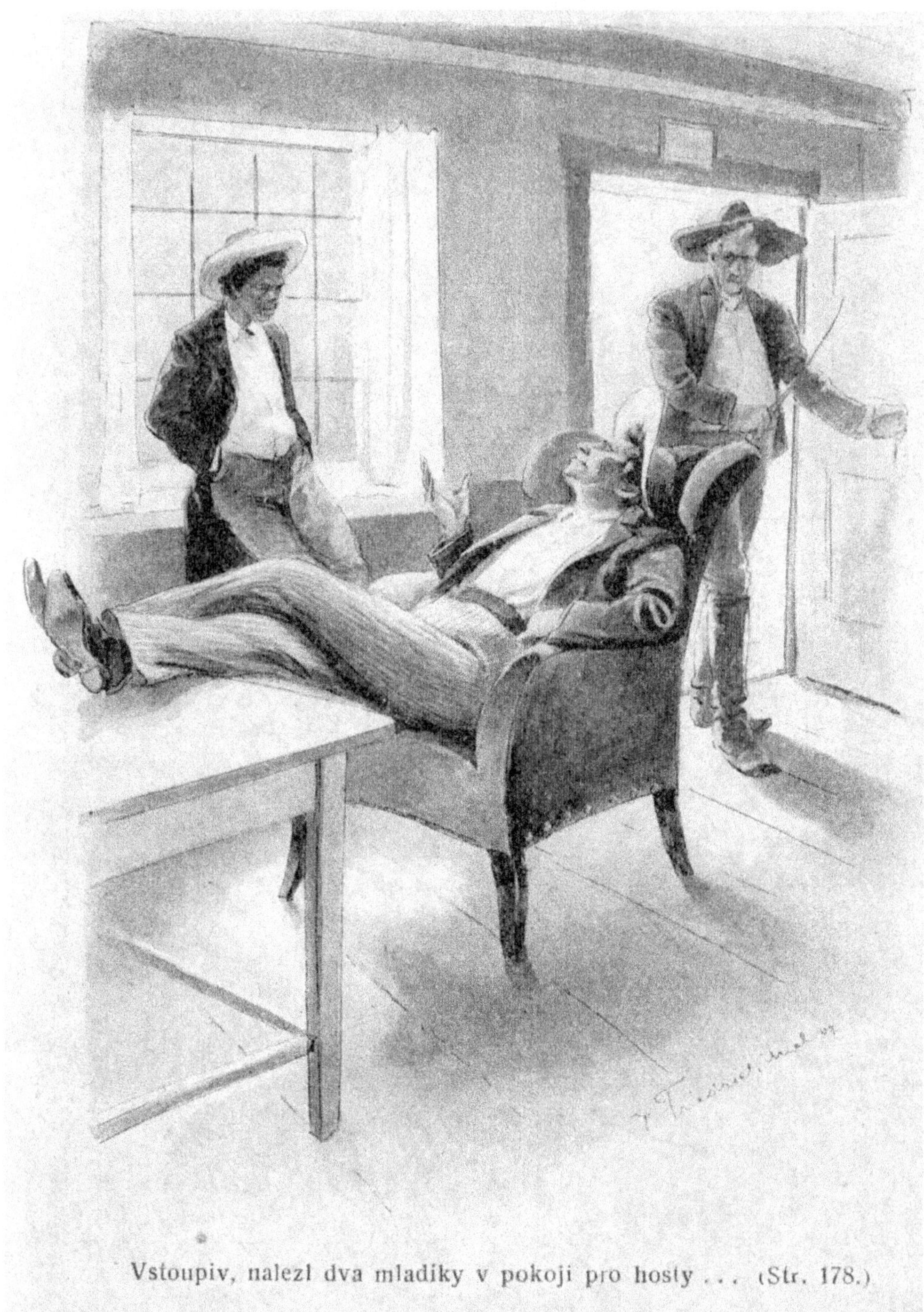

Vstoupiv, nalezl dva mladiky v pokoji pro hosty ... (Str. 178.)

Image 22/29. Page 185.
Vstoupiv, nalezl dva mladiky v pokoji pro hosty... (str. 178)
(Entering, he found two young men in a guest room ... p. 178)
SH-JF93

Josef Friedrich – A Study in Scarlet
(Mstitel, Vilímek, Prague 1907)

Na skále, strmící nad stezkou, stála osamělá stráž . . . (Str. 195.)

Image 23/29. Page 193.
Na skále, strmící nad stezkou, stála osamělá stráž... (str. 195)
(On a rock, steeply above the trail, stood alone guard ... p. 195)
SH-JF94

Josef Friedrich – A Study in Scarlet
(Mstitel, Vilímek, Prague 1907)

Nápis na papíru byl krátký, ale pověděl vše . . . (Str. 205.)

Image 24/29. Page 201.
Nápis na papíru byl Krátký, ale pověděl vše... (str. 205)
(The paper was written by Kratky, but he knew everything... p. 205)
SH-JF95

Josef Friedrich – A Study in Scarlet
(Mstitel, Vilímek, Prague 1907)

. . . přikročil k němé, bělostné postavě . . . (Str. 210.)

Image 25/29. Page 209.
Prikrocil k neme belostne postave…(Str. 210)
(He approached a silent white figure…p. 210)
SH-JF96

Josef Friedrich – A Study in Scarlet
(Mstitel, Vilímek, Prague 1907)

Mluvil klidně a methodicky . . . (Str. 224.)

Image 26/29. Page 221.
Mluvil klidně a methodicky... (Str. 224)
(He spoke calmly and methodically ... p. 224)
SH-JF97

Josef Friedrich – A Study in Scarlet
(Mstitel, Vilímek, Prague 1907)

. . . spatřiv můj vůz, najal jej a vsedl dovnitř . . . (Str. 231.)

Image 27/29. Page 229.
... spatřiv můj vůz, najal jej a vsedl dovnitř... (Str. 231)
(... saw a cab, hired it, and got in ... p. 231)
SH-JF98

Josef Friedrich – A Study in Scarlet
(Mstitel, Vilímek, Prague 1907)

. . . řekl jsem mu, že udeřila hodina, kdy se má zodpovídati . . . (Str. 239.)

Image 28/29. Page 237.
. Řekl jsem mu, že uderila hodina, kdy se má zodpovidati..(str. 239)
... I told him that the hour had come to answer ... p. 239)
SH-JF99

Josef Friedrich – A Study in Scarlet
(Mstitel, Vilímek, Prague 1907)

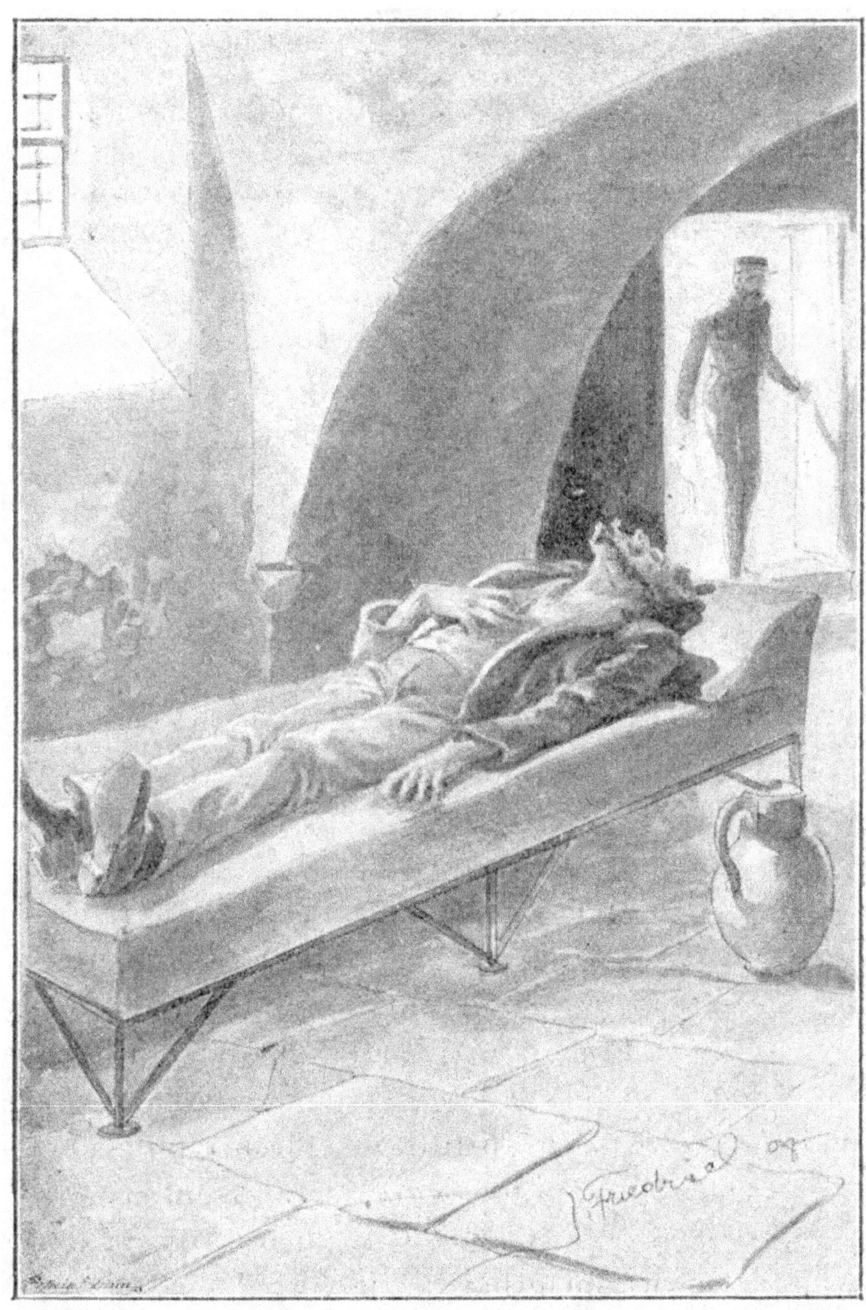

. . . byl nalezen mrtev ráno ve své cele . . . (Str. 243.

Image 29/29. Page 245.
... byl nalezen mrtev ráno ve své cele... (str.243)
(... was found dead in the morning ... p.243)
SH-JF100

Solar D'Alba

Born 1876 in Spain
Died in France

Started out as a humorous illustrator for French comic Le Tutu in 1901. He subsequently illustrated for L'Illustré National, La Vie Amusante, and La Gaîté Gauloise. His drawings appeared in Mes Cartes Postales, Jeudi de la Jeunesse, Les Images Pour Rire and La Vie de Garnison. During World War I, he contributed to Nos Poilus, Le Carnet de la Semaine and La Rampe. No work by

He produced six illustrations for the French Newspaper Mon Dimanche (My Sunday) in a six-part translation of The Red-Headed League (La Ligue des têtes rouges)

These are newspaper images and so the quality is not as good as book illustrations.

Date	Issue	# images
16th August 1903	37	2
23rd August 1903	38	1
30th August 1903	39	1
6th September 1903	40	0
13th September 1903	41	1
20th September 1903	42	1

Solar D'Alba - La Ligue des têtes rouges 16th August 1903

Image 1/6. Page 170. La Ligue Des têtes Rouges (The League of Red Heads) Title
SH-SDA1

Solar D’Alba - La Ligue des têtes rouges 16th August 1903

JE LUS AVEC ATTENTION DANS LA « MORNING CHRONICLE » L'EXTRAORDINAIRE ANNONCE DE LA LIGUE.

Image 2/6. Page 170. Je lus avec attention dans la “Morning Chronicle” l’extraordinaire annonce de la ligue. (I read with attention in the “Morning Chronicle” the extraordinary announcement of the league.)
SH-SDA2

Solar D'Alba - La Ligue des têtes rouges 23rd August 1903

JE FUS PRÉSENTÉ PAR MON EMPLOYÉ ET MES CHEVEUX FURENT L'OBJET D'UN EXAMEN SÉRIEUX

Image 3/6. Page 186. Je fus présenté par mon employé et mes cheveus furent l'object d'un examen serieux (I was introduced by my employee and my hair was the object of a serious examination.)
SH-SDA3

Solar D'Alba - La Ligue des têtes rouges 30th August 1903

LA MAISON OCCUPÉE PAR M. JABEZ WILSON ET QUE VISITERA M. HOLMES ET SON AMI.

Image 4/6. Page 202. La maison occupée par M. Jabez Wilson et que visitera M. Holmes et son ami. (The house occupied by Mr. Jabez Wilson, and which will be visited by Mr. Holmes and his friend.)
SH-SDA4

M. HOLMES ET SES COMPAGNONS ATTENDENT LES VOLEURS DANS LA CAVE DE LA BANQUE

Image 5/6. Page 234. M. Holmes et ses compagnons attendant les voleurs dans la cave de la banque. (Mr. Holmes and his companions waiting for the robbers in the cellar of the bank.) *SH-SDA5*

Solar D’Alba - La Ligue des têtes rouges 20th September 1903

L’ARRESTATION DANS LA CAVE DE LA BANQUE
DU CÉLÈBRE CAMBRIOLEUR, JOHN CLAY.

Image 6/6. Page 250. L'arrestation dans le sous-sol de la banque du célèbre cambrioleur, John Clay. (The arrest in the basement of the bank of notorious burglar, John Clay.)
SH-SDA6

Charles R. Macauley

Born in Canton, Ohio on 19th March 1871
Died in St. Vincent's Hospital,
Manhattan on 24th November 1934

Charles R. Macauley started his newspaper work with the Cleveland News, when he won a drawing prize offered by the newspaper for the best portrayal of the spirit of Thanksgiving. He made contributions to this paper as well as the Cleveland World, Cleveland Plain Dealer and Cleveland Leader.
He migrated to Philadelphia and spent time on the Inquirer and then went to the New York Herald and later the New York World, succeeding the late C. G. Bush.
It was said that his drawings never lacked vigour, were free from venom and many public men, who were the target of his keen thrusts asked him for his original drawings, he seldom refused.
In 1905 he produced 13 illustrations for the McClure, Phillips & Co.'s The Return of Sherlock Holmes

- The Empty House
- The Norwood Builder
- The Dancing Men
- The Solitary Cyclist
- The Priory School
- Black Peter
- Charles Augustus Milverton
- The Six Napoleons
- The Three Students
- The Golden Pince-Nez
- The Missing Three-Quarters
- The Abbey Grange
- The Second Stain

Charles R. Macauley – The Norwood Builder 1905

MR. JONAS OLDACRE

Image 1/13. Frontispiece. (NORW) Mr. Jonas Oldacre
SH-CRM1

Charles R. Macauley – The Empty House 1905

I KNOCKED DOWN SEVERAL BOOKS WHICH HE WAS CARRYING

Image 2/13. Page 8. (EMPT) I knocked down several books which he was carrying.
SH-CRM2

Charles R. Macauley – The Dancing Men 1905

"THREE DAYS LATER A MESSAGE WAS LEFT UNDER A PEBBLE UPON THE SUN-DIAL"

Image 3/13. Page 70. (DANC) Three days later a message was left under a pebble upon the sun-dial"
SH-CRM3

Charles R. Macauley – The Solitary Cyclist 1905

A SOLITARY CYCLIST WAS COMING TOWARDS US

Image 4/13. Page 110. (SOLI) A solitary cyclist was coming towards us
SH-CRM4

Charles R. Macauley – The Priory School 1905

AN INSTANT LATER, HIS FEET WERE ON MY SHOULDERS

Image 5/13. Page 148. (PRIO) An instant later, his feet were on my shoulders
SH-CRM5

Charles R. Macauley – Black Peter 1905

"I GOT A SHAKE WHEN I PUT MY HEAD INTO THAT LITTLE HOUSE"

Image 6/13. Page 164. (BLAC) "I got a shake when I put my head into that little house"
SH-CRM6

Charles R. Macauley – Charles Augustus Milverton 1905

HE FELL FORWARD UPON THE TABLE, COUGHING FURIOUSLY AND CLAWING AMONG THE PAPERS

Image 7/13. Page 206. (CHAS) He fell forward upon the table coughing furiously and clawing among the papers.
SH-CRM7

Charles R. Macauley – The Six Napoleons 1905

WE SAW THAT HE CARRIED SOMETHING WHITE UNDER HIS ARM

Image 8/13. Page 228. (SIXN) We saw that he carried something under his arm
SH-CRM8

Charles R. Macauley – The Three Students 1905

THREE YELLOW SQUARES OF LIGHT SHONE ABOVE US IN THE GATHERING GLOOM

Image 9/13. Page 250. (3STU) Three yellow squares of light shone above us in the gathering gloom
SH-CRM9

IT WAS A GAUNT, AQUILINE FACE WHICH WAS TURNED TOWARDS US

Image 10/13. Page 275. (GOLD) It was a gaunt, aquiline face which was turned towards us
SH-CRM10

Charles R. Macauley – The Missing Three-Quarter 1905

I CAUGHT A GLIMPSE OF DR. ARMSTRONG WITHIN

Image 11/13. Page 314. (MISS) I caught a glimpse of Dr. Armstrong within
SH-CRM11

Charles R. Macauley – The Abbey Grange 1905

"THESE THREE GLASSES UPON THE SIDEBOARD HAVE BEEN UNTOUCHED, I SUPPOSE?"

Image 12/13. Page 330. (ABBE) "These three glasses upon the sideboard have been untouched, I suppose?"
SH-CRM12

Charles R. Macauley – The Second Stain 1905

HE FOUND HOLMES LEANING LANGUIDLY AGAINST THE MANTELPIECE

Image 13/13. Page 372. (SECO) He found Holmes leaning languidly against the mantelpiece
SH-CRM13

John Richard Flanagan Error! Bookmark not defined.

Born 23rd July 1895 in Sydney, NSW, Australia
Died 12th December 1964

The eldest of 4 siblings, he did 8 illustrations for two Sherlock Holmes stories, The Three Garridebs(4) and The Illustrious Client(4), for Colliers Magazine in 1924.

Image 1/4. Page 5. "It only needs one more Garrideb – and surely, we can find one."
SH-JRF1

John R. Flanagan – The Three Garridebs - Collier's 25th October 1924

Image 2/4. Page 6. The man in the open trap door whisked out a revolver and fired
SH-JRF2

John R. Flanagan – The Three Garridebs - Collier's 25th October 1924

Image 3/4. Page 7. Killer Evans after shooting Dr. Watson
SH-JRF3

John R. Flanagan – The Three Garridebs - Collier's 25th October 1924

"A printing press—a counterfeiter's outfit," said Holmes

Image 4/4. Page 36. "A printing press – a counterfeiter's outfit." Said Holmes.
SH-JRF4

John Richard Flanagan – The Illustrious Client - Collier's 8th November 1924

"It needs careful handling, Watson. A set of this would be worth a king's ransom

Image 1/4. Page 5. "It needs careful handling, Watson. A set of this would be worth a king's ransom
SH-JRF5

John R. Flanagan – The Illustrious Client - Collier's 8th November 1924

Image 2/4. Page 6. His air of romance and mystery put the whole sex at his mercy
SH-JRF6

Image 3/4. Page 7. In the great drawing-room a lady awaited us, demure and remote as a snow image on a mountain
SH-JRF7

Image 4/4. Page 30. Shinwell Johnson's vivid black eyes were the only external sign of the very cunning mind within
SH-JRF8

San Francisco Call

The San Francisco Call /The Sunday Call Daily newspaper was set up in 1856 as the Daily Morning Call. It was renamed in 1895 and was purchased by William Randolph Heart in 1913, but it is in 1905 that we will be concerning ourselves, when they published 25 Sherlock Holmes stories with various illustrators and 55 illustrations.

No.	Date	Story	Ills.	Artist
1	05.03.1905	EMPT	5	Stanley E. Armstrong
2	12.03.1905	NORW	4	R. Thomson
3	19.03.1905	DANC	4	R. Thomson
4	26.03.1905	SOLI	3	Reginald G. Russom
5	02.04.1905	PRIO	3	Walter W. Francis
6	09.04.1905	BLAC	4	Stanley E. Armstrong
7	16.04.1905	CHAS	3	Stanley E. Armstrong
8	23.04.1905	SIXN	4	R. Thomson
9	30.04.1905	3STU	2	R. Thomson
10	07.05.1905	GOLD	1	Stanley E. Armstrong + 1 map
11	14.05.1905	MISS	2	R. Thomson
12	21.05.1905	ABBE	1	Reginald G. Russom
13	28.05.1905	SECO	1	Walter W. Francis & Stanley E. Armstrong
14	03.09.1905	ENGR	2	Walter W. Francis
15	10.09.1905	SPEC	2	Walter W. Francis
16	17.09.1905	BERY	2	Walter W. Francis
17	24.09.1905	COPP	2	Walter W. Francis
18	01.10.1905	IDEN	2	Walter W. Francis
19	08.10.1905	REDH	1	Stanley E. Armstrong
20	15.10.1905	NOBL	1	Walter W. Francis
21	22.10.1905	SILV	2	Stanley E. Armstrong
22	29.10.1905	YELL	1	Walter W. Francis
23	05.11.1905	STOC	1	Stanley E. Armstrong
24	12.11.1905	GLOR	1	Walter W. Francis
25	19.11.1905	MUSG	1	Stanley E. Armstrong

We will present these stories and illustrations in published date order, Yes, I know this will mean that the artist's works are not all together and will be scattered over the next 61 pages, I also break with convention with my arbitrary decision to show whole pages with combined images together and then the individual parts, and I know this will annoy any purists as my image count will be 'wrong', but feel justified because this enabled me to show some of the smaller images at a decent quality..
But first some details about the artists, who are going to be mentioned in this next section, in alphabetic order.

Stanley Edward Armstrong

Born 11th July 1873 in Muir, Michigan
Died 16th March 1949 in San Francisco

American Cartoonist and illustrator who attended the Mark Hopkins' Institute of Art in San Francisco. He worked on a number of cartoons including, Jerry the Juggler, 'Slim Jim and the Force'. Moving back to California in the 1920s, he was a cartoonist and illustrator for the Danger Trail and Ace-High Magazine.

He produced 20 illustrations of Sherlock Holmes in the San Francisco Call.

Date	No. of Images	
5th March 1905	The Empty House	5
9th April 1905	Black Peter	5
16th April 1905	Charles Augustus Milverton	3
7th May 1905	The Golden Pince-Nez	1
28th May 1905	The Second Stain	½
8th October 1905	The Red-Headed League	1
22nd October 1905	Silver Blaze	2
5th November 1905	Stockbroker's Clerk	1
19th November 1905	The Musgrave Ritual	1

Walter W. Francis

Born 1846 New York

In his 30s Francis was a miner, working in the Bodie, Ca mines, but in 1890 he made a life change and settled in San Francisco where he studied at the Mark Hopkins Art institute before becoming an illustrator for the Chronical and the San Francisco Call.
He Illustrated 14 of the Sherlock Holmes Stories

Date	No. of Images	
2nd April 1905	The Priory School	3
28th May 1905	The Second Stain	½
3rd September 1905	The Engineer's thumb	2
10th September 1905	The Speckled Band	2
17th September 1905	The Beryl Coronet	2
24th September 1905	The Copper Beeches	2
1st October 1905	A Case of Identity	2
8th October 1905	The Red-Headed League	1
15th October 1905	The Noble Bachelor	1
29th October 1905	The Yellow Face	1
12th November 1905	The Gloria Scott	1

Reginald Gordon Russom

Born 1887 or 1877 or 1880 Sydney, NSW Australia, depending on resource.
Died 1952 in Newcastle, NSW, Australia
Left Australia at the age of nineteen and moved to San Francisco where he was a Cartoonist and illustrator for a number of publications.
He did 4 illustrations in total, 3 for the adventure of the Solitary cyclist and 1 for the Abbey Grange for the San Francisco Call in 1905

Date	No. of Images	
26th March 1905	The Solitary Cyclist	3
21st May 1905	The Abbey Grange	1

R. Thomson

Sorry no biographical data was found for this artist, however, here are details of his Sherlock Holmes stories illustrations.

Date	No. of Images	
12th March 1905	The Norwood Builder	4
19th March 1905	The Dancing men	4
23rd April 1905	The Six Napoleons	3
30th April 1905	The Three Students	2
14th May 1905	The Missing Three-Quarter	2

Stanley E. Armstrong - San Francisco Call:Empty House, The 5th Mar 1905

Supplement to THE CALL

THE SUNDAY CALL MAGAZINE

San Francisco Sunday March 5 1905

THE RETURN OF SHERLOCK HOLMES

BY A CONAN DOYLE

THE ADVENTURE OF THE EMPTY HOUSE

No. 1

Image 1/7. Front Page

SH-SEA1

Image 2/7. Front Page, top left. His sharp, wizened face peering out from a frame of white hair.
SH-SEA2

Stanley E. Armstrong - San Francisco Call:Empty House, The 5th Mar 1905

Image 3/7. Front Page, Middle. When I turned again, Sherlock Holmes was standing smiling at me across my study table.
SH-SEA3

Stanley E. Armstrong - San Francisco Call:Empty House, The 5th Mar 1905

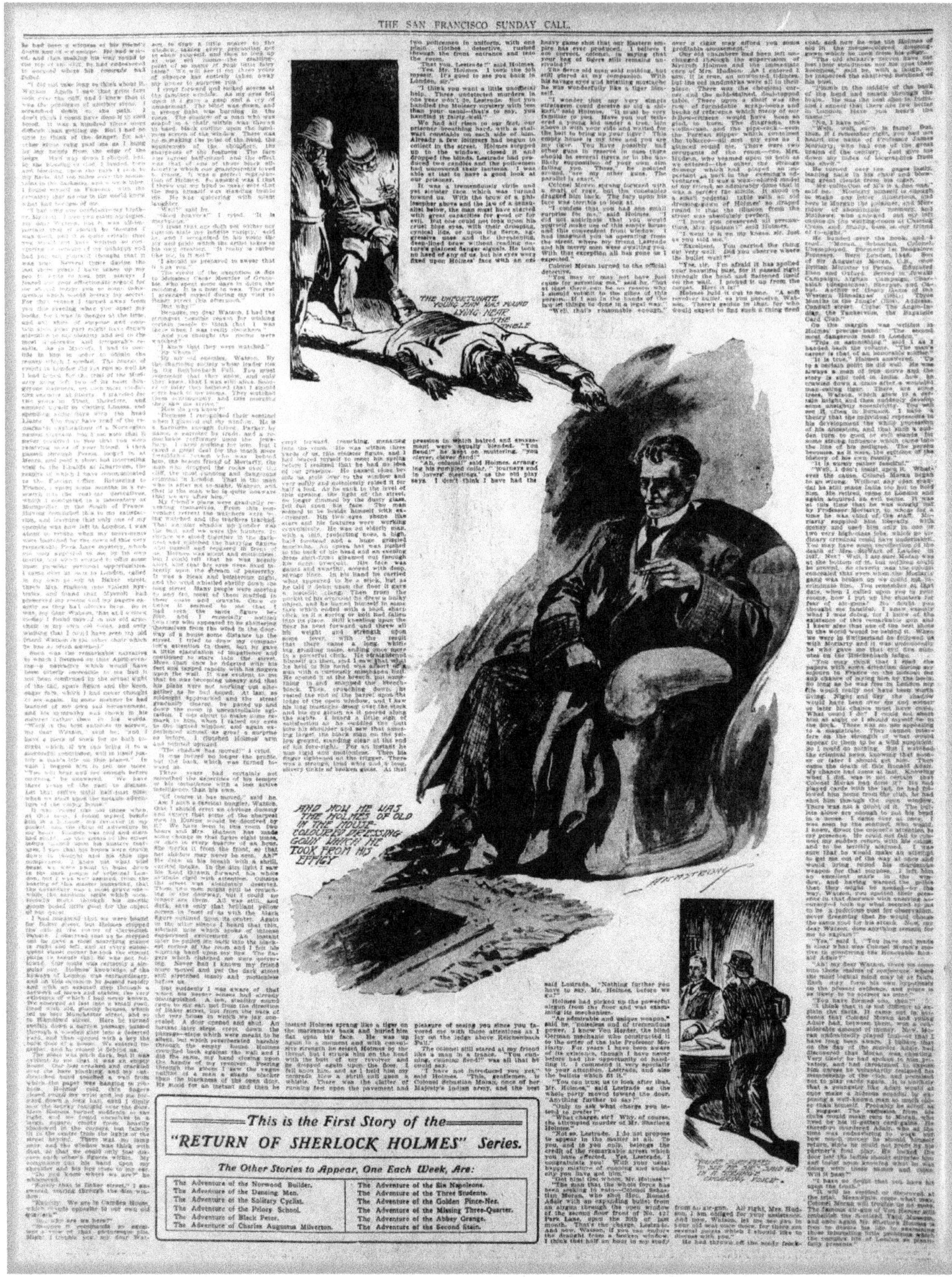

Image 4/7. Page 2,
SH-SEA4

Image 5/7. Page 2, Top. The unfortunate young man was found lying near the table.
SH-SEA5

Image 6/7. Page 2, Middle. And now he was the Holmes of old in the mouse-coloured dressing-gown which he took from his effigy.
SH-SEA6

Stanley E. Armstrong - San Francisco Call:Empty House, The 5th Mar 1905

Image 7/7. Page 2, Bottom. "You're surprised to see me, sir," said he, in a strange, croaking voice.
SH-SEA7

R. Thomson - San Francisco Call:Norwood Builder, The 12th Mar 1905

Supplement to THE CALL

THE SUNDAY CALL MAGAZINE

San Francisco Sunday MARCH 12th 1905

THE RETURN OF SHERLOCK HOLMES

The ADVENTURE of the NORWOOD BUILDER.

BY A. CONAN DOYLE

No 2

Image 1/6. Front Page

SH-RT1

R. Thomson - San Francisco Call:Norwood Builder, The 12th Mar 1905

Image 2/6. Front Page, Left. "Look at that with your magnifying glass, Mr. Holmes."
SH-RT2

R. Thomson - San Francisco Call:Norwood Builder, The 12th Mar 1905

Image 3/6. Front Page, Middle. A door flew open out of what appeared to be solid wall, and a little man darted out.
SH-RT3

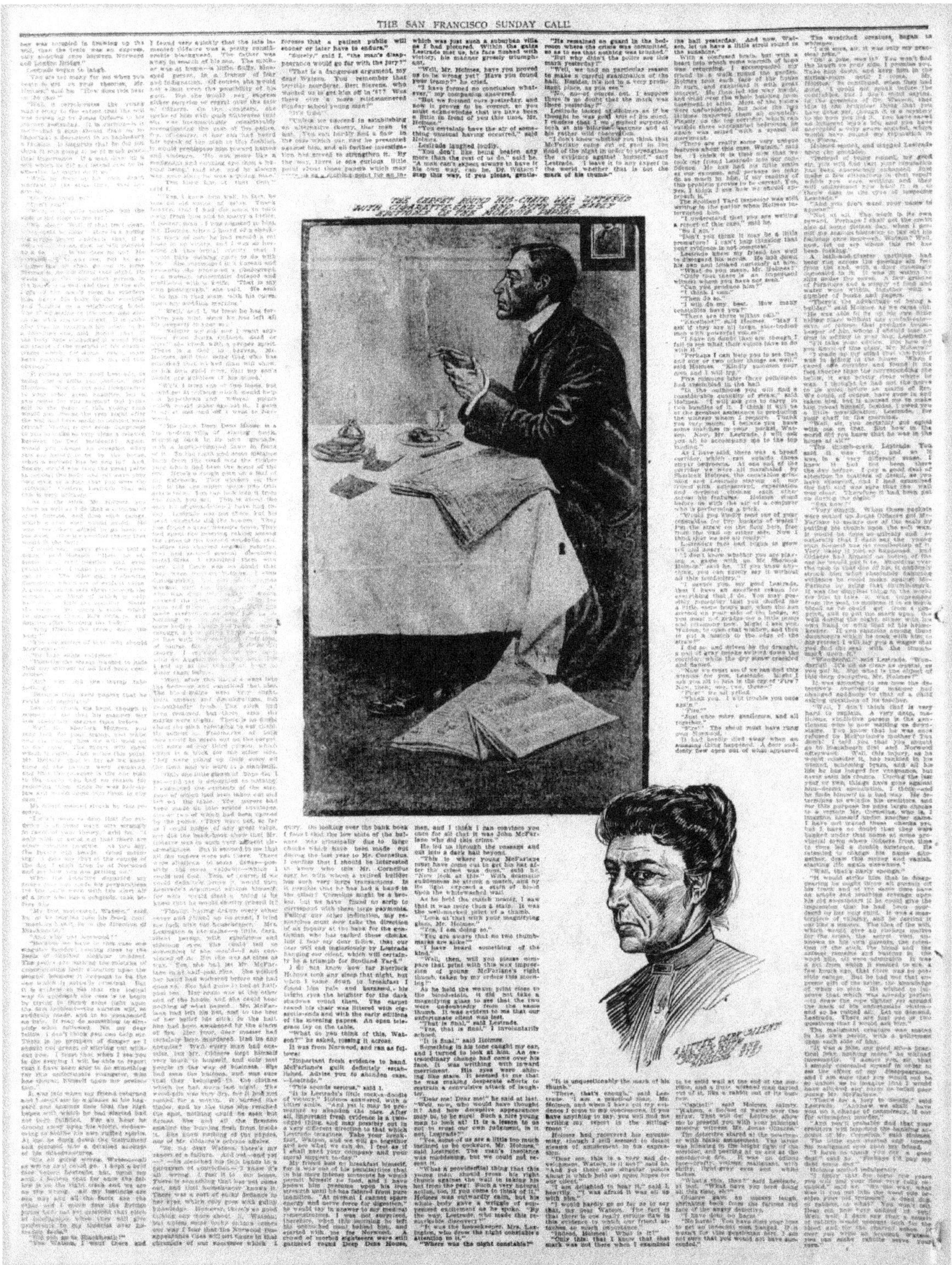

THE SAN FRANCISCO SUNDAY CALL

"He remained on guard in the bedroom where the crime was committed, so as to see that nothing was touched."

"But why didn't the police see this mark yesterday?"

"Well, we had no particular reason to make a careful examination of the hall. Besides, it's not in a very prominent place, as you see."

[illegible]

Image 4/6. Page 2.
SH-RT4

Image 5/6. Page 2, left. The carpet round his chair was littered with cigarette ends and with the early editions of the morning papers.
SH-RT5

R. Thomson - San Francisco Call:Norwood Builder, The 12th Mar 1905

Image 6/6. Front Page, right. A little dark silent person with suspicious and sidelong eyes.
SH-RT6

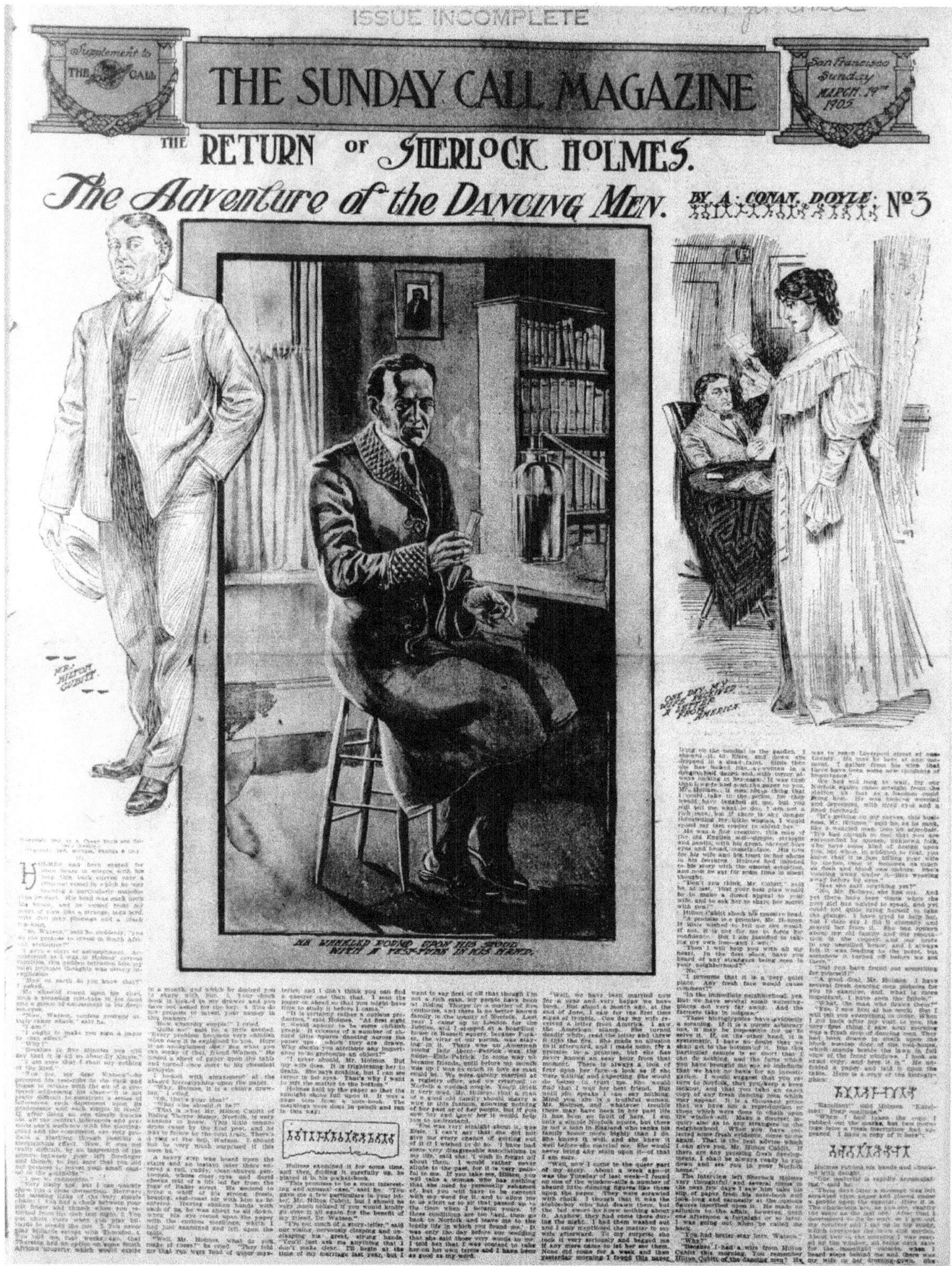

ISSUE INCOMPLETE

Supplement to THE CALL

THE SUNDAY CALL MAGAZINE

San Francisco Sunday March 19th 1905

THE RETURN OF SHERLOCK HOLMES.

The Adventure of the Dancing Men.

BY A. CONAN DOYLE. No 3

MR. HILTON CUBITT

HE WHEELED ROUND UPON HIS STOOL WITH A TEST-TUBE IN HIS HAND.

ONE DAY MY WIFE RECEIVED A LETTER FROM AMERICA

Image 1/7. Front Page

SH-RT7

R. Thomson - San Francisco Call:Dancing Men, The 19th Mar 1905

Image 2/5. Front Page, Left. Mr. Hilton Cubitt
SH-RT8

Image 3/5. Front Page, Middle. He wheeled round upon his stool with a test-tube in his hand.
SH-RT9

Image 4/5. Front Page, right. One day, my wife received a letter from America.
SH-RT10

R. Thomson - San Francisco Call:Dancing Men, The 19th Mar 1905

Image 5/5. Page 2. She came down and brought money with her, trying to bribe me to go.
SH-RT11

Reginald G. Russom - San Francisco Call:Solitary Cyclist, The 26th Mar 1905

Supplement to THE CALL

THE SUNDAY CALL MAGAZINE

San Francisco Sunday March 26th 1905

THE RETURN OF SHERLOCK HOLMES. No. 4

BY A. CONAN DOYLE.

The Adventure of the Solitary Cyclist.

"He made odious love to me."

Image 1/4. Front Page.
SH-RGR1

Reginald G. Russom - San Francisco Call:Solitary Cyclist, The 26th Mar 1905

Image 2/4. Front Page. Left. Miss. Violet Smith
SH-RGR2

Reginald G. Russom - San Francisco Call:Solitary Cyclist, The 26th Mar 1905

Image 3/4. Front Page. Right. "He made odious love to me."
SH-RGR3

Reginald G. Russom - San Francisco Call:Solitary Cyclist, The 26th Mar 1905

Image 4/4. Page 2. "Pull up, I say or by George, I'll put a bullet into your horse."
SH-RGR4

Walter W. Francis - San Francisco Call:Priory School, The 2nd Apr 1905

Supplement to THE CALL

THE SUNDAY CALL MAGAZINE

San Francisco Sunday April 2 1905.

The Return of Sherlock Holmes

No.5 The Adventure of the Priory School

by A.CONAN DOYLE

Image 1/4. Front Page.
SH-WWF1

Walter W. Francis - San Francisco Call:Priory School, The 2nd Apr 1905

Image 2/4. Front Page, Top Left. Lord Saltire
SH-WWF2

Walter W. Francis - San Francisco Call:Priory School, The 2nd Apr 1905

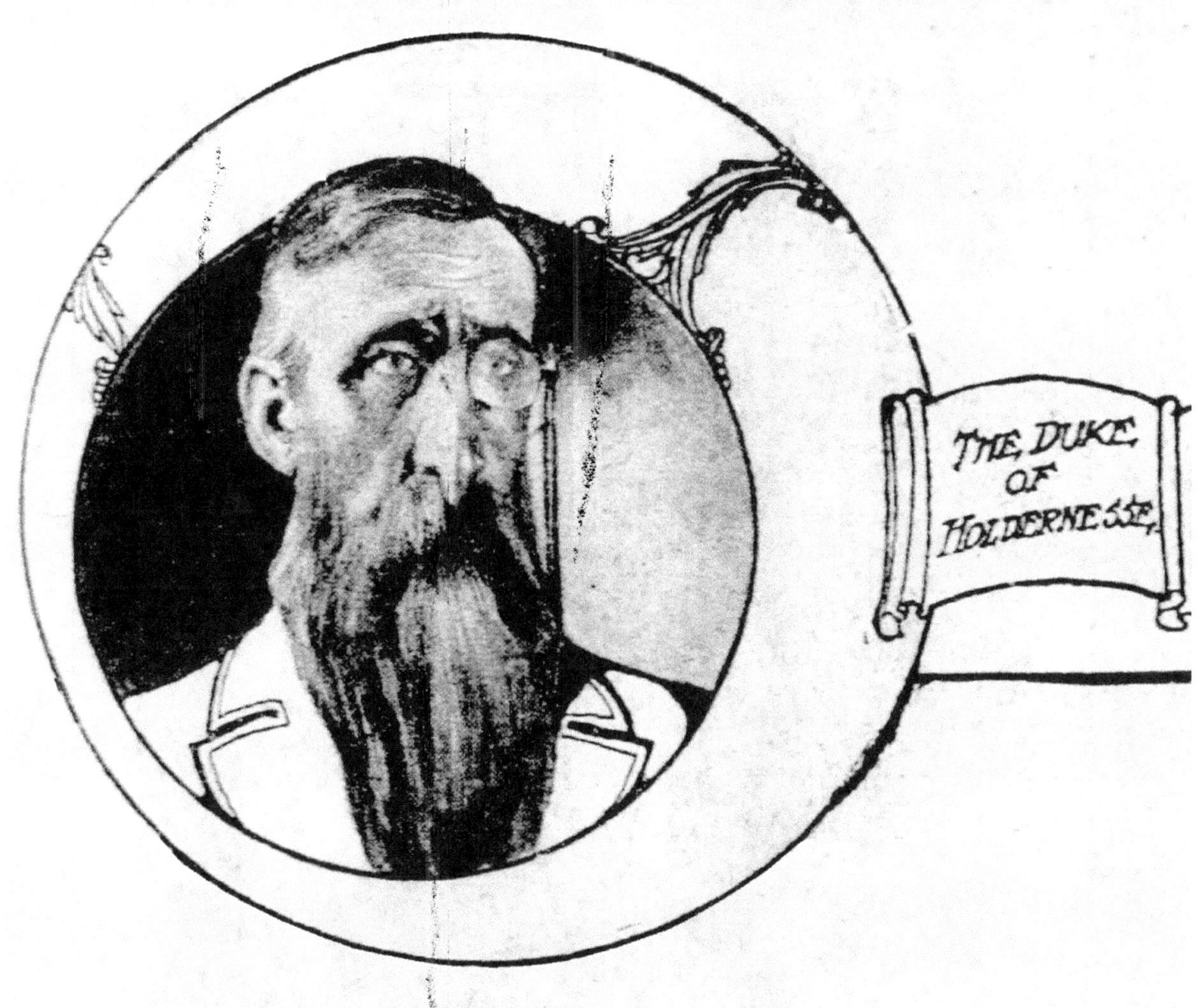

Image 3/4. Front Page, Top Middle. The Duke of Holdernesse
SH-WWF3

Image 4/4. Front Page, Bottom. "You infernal spies! The man cried. "What are you doing there?"
SH-WWF4

Stanley E. Armstrong - San Francisco Call:Black Peter 9th Apr 1905

Supplement to THE CALL

THE SUNDAY CALL MAGAZINE

San Francisco Sunday APRIL 9 1905

The Return of Sherlock Holmes

THE ADVENTURE OF BLACK PETER

BY A. CONAN DOYLE

No 6

THE SECOND MAN WAS A LONG DRIED UP CREATURE WITH DARK HAIR AND SALLOW CHEEK

A FIERCE BULL-DOG FACE WAS FRAMED IN A TANGLE OF HAIR AND BEARD

Image 1/6. Front Page.
SH-SEA8

Stanley E. Armstrong - San Francisco Call:Black Peter 9th Apr 1905

Image 2/6. Front Page. Top Left Caption. The second man was a long dried up creature with lank hair and sallow cheek.
SH-SEA9

Stanley E. Armstrong - San Francisco Call:Black Peter 9th Apr 1905

Image 3/6. Front Page. Middle Top panel
SH-SEA10

Stanley E. Armstrong - San Francisco Call:Black Peter 9th Apr 1905

Image 4/6. Front Page. Top Left
SH-SEA11

Stanley E. Armstrong - San Francisco Call:Black Peter 9th Apr 1905

Image 5/6. Front Page. Middle. A fierce bull-dog face was framed in a tangle of hair and beard.
SH-SEA12

Stanley E. Armstrong - San Francisco Call:Black Peter 9th Apr 1905

Image 6/6. Page 2. Middle. I have never seen any human being who appeared to be in such a pitiable fright
SH-SEA13

Stanley E. Armstrong - San Francisco Call:Charles Augustus Milverton 16th Apr 1905

Image 1/5. Front Page.
SH-SEA14

Image 2/5. Front Page.
SH-SEA15

Stanley E. Armstrong - San Francisco Call:Charles Augustus Milverton
16th Apr 1905

Image 3/5. Front Page. Right. For half an hour Holmes worked with concentrated energy.
SH-SEA16

Stanley E. Armstrong - San Francisco Call:Charles Augustus Milverton 16th Apr 1905

Image 5/5. Page 2. Right in front of us and almost within our reach, was the broad rounded back of Milverton

SH-SEA17

R. Thomson - San Francisco Call:Six Napoleons, The 23rd Apr 1905

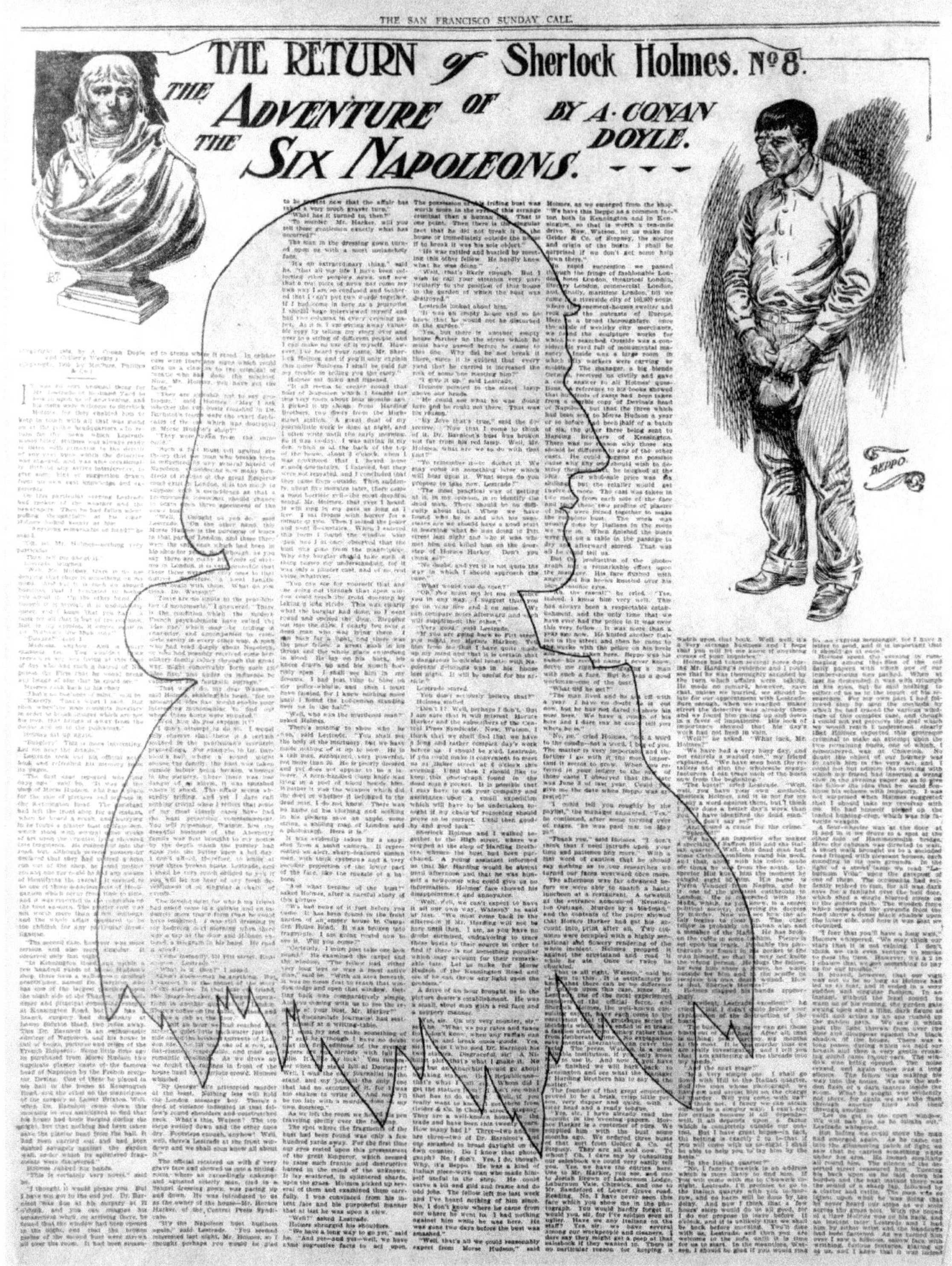

THE SAN FRANCISCO SUNDAY CALL.

THE RETURN of Sherlock Holmes. No 8.

THE ADVENTURE OF THE SIX NAPOLEONS.

BY A. CONAN DOYLE.

Image 1/4. Page 1.

SH-RT8

R. Thomson - San Francisco Call:Six Napoleons, The 23rd Apr 1905

Image 2/4. Page 1,Top Left. One of the Six Napoleons
SH-RT9

R. Thomson - San Francisco Call:Six Napoleons, The 23rd Apr 1905

Image 3/4. Page 1,Top Right. Beppo
SH-RT10

R. Thomson - San Francisco Call:Six Napoleons, The 23rd Apr 1905

Image 4/4. Page 2.The man was so intent upon what he was doing that he never heard our footsteps.
SH-RT11

Image 1/2. Page 1. I was aware that someone had rummaged among my papers.
SH-RT12

Image 2/2. Page 2. A tall, young fellow opened the door and made us welcome.
SH-RT13

Stanley E. Armstrong - San Francisco Call:Golden Pince-Nez, The 7th May 1905

Image 1/1. Front Page. It was a gaunt aquiline face which was turned towards us., with piercing dark eyes, in deep hollows under overhung and tufted brows
SH-SEA18

R. Thomson - San Francisco Call:Missing Three-Quarter, The 14th May 1905

Supplement to THE CALL

THE SUNDAY CALL MAGAZINE

San Francisco Sunday May 14th 1905

THE RETURN OF SHERLOCK HOLMES.

THE ADVENTURE OF THE MISSING THREE-QUARTER.

BY A·CONAN DOYLE.

IN HALF AN HOUR, WE WERE CLEAR OF THE TOWN AND HASTENING DOWN A COUNTRY ROAD.

Image 1/3. Front Page. In half an hour, we were clear of the town and hastening down a country road.
SH-RT14

Image 2/3. Front Page. Top. Pompey the Dog.
SH-RT15

R. Thomson - San Francisco Call:Missing Three-Quarter, The 14th May 1905

Image 3/3. Front Page. Right. In half an hour, we were clear of the town and hastening down a country road.
SH-RT16

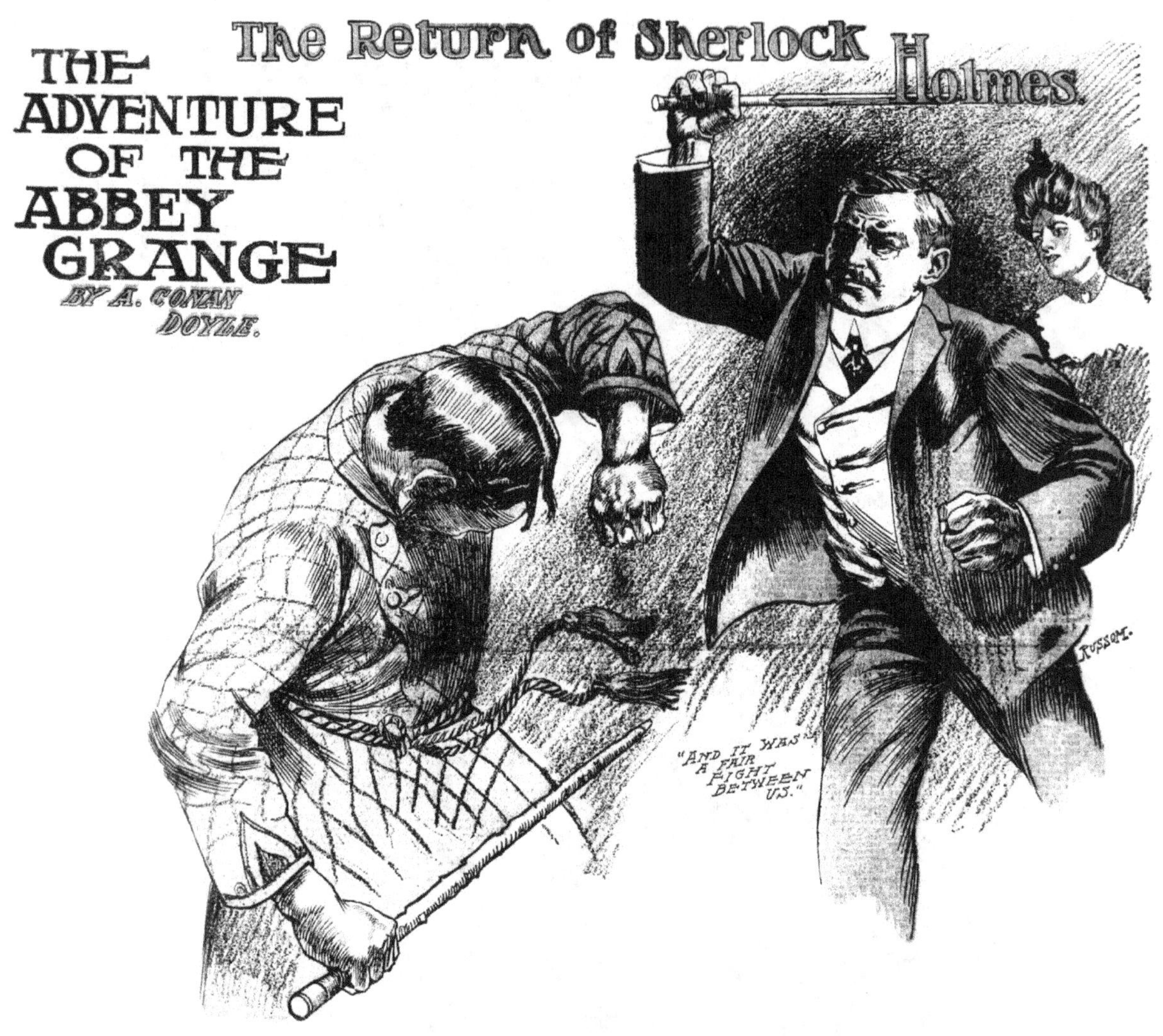

Image 1/1. Front Page. "And it was a fair fight between us."
SH-RGR5

Stanley E. Armstrong & Walter W. Francis - San Francisco Call:Second Stain, The 28th May 1905

Image 1/1. Front Page. "It was empty."
SH-SEA19 & SH-WWF5

THE SAN FRANCISCO SUNDAY CALL.

THE BEST OF THE SHERLOCK HOLMES STORIES

The Adventure of the Engineer's Thumb

BY

A. CONAN DOYLE.

Image 1/3. Front Page.
SH-WWF6

Walter W. Francis - San Francisco Call:Engineer's Thumb, The 3rd September 1905

Image 2/3. Front Page. Colonel Lysander Stark. "I do not think that I have ever seen so thin a man."
SH-WWF7

Walter W. Francis - San Francisco Call:Engineer's Thumb, The 3rd September 1905

" VERY WELL,' SAID HE, 'YOU SHALL KNOW ALL ABOUT THE MACHINE.'"

Image 3/3. Front Page. "Very well" said he, "You shall know all about the machine."
SH-WWF8

Supplement to THE CALL

THE SUNDAY CALL MAGAZINE

San Francisco Sunday Sept. 10. 1905

The Best of the Sherlock Holmes Stories

THE ADVENTURE OF THE SPECKLED BAND

BY A. CONAN DOYLE

"THE BAND! THE SPECKLED BAND!" WHISPERED HOLMES.

Image 1/3. Front Page.

SH-WWF9

Walter W. Francis - San Francisco Call:Speckled Band, The 10th September 1905

Image 2/3. Front Page. "There is no mystery, my dear madam" said he?
SH-WWF10

Walter W. Francis - San Francisco Call:Speckled Band, The 10th September 1905

Image 3/3. Front Page. "The band! The Speckled Band!" Whispered Holmes."
SH-WWF11

Supplement to THE CALL

THE SUNDAY CALL MAGAZINE

San Francisco Sunday Sept. 17 1905

The Best of the Sherlock Holmes Stories

The Adventure of the Beryl Coronet.

by A. CONAN DOYLE

Image 1/3. Front Page.
SH-WWF12

Walter W. Francis - San Francisco Call:Beryl Coronet, The 17th September 1905

Image 2/3. Front Page, Left.
SH-WWF13

Walter W. Francis - San Francisco Call:Beryl Coronet, The 17th September 1905

Image 3/3. Front Page, right. "And with a scream, fell down senseless on the floor."
SH-WWF14

Walter W. Francis - San Francisco Call:Copper Beeches, The 24th September 1905

Supplement to THE CALL

THE SUNDAY CALL MAGAZINE

San Francisco Sunday Sept. 24. 1905

THE BEST OF THE SHERLOCK HOLMES STORIES

The Adventure of the Copper Beeches

by A. CONAN DOYLE

Image 1/3. Front Page.
SH-WWF15

Walter W. Francis - San Francisco Call:Copper Beeches, The 24th September 1905

Image 2/3. Front Page bottom left. "A very fat and burly man, with a heavy stick in his hand."
SH-WWF16

Image 3/3. Front Page Top Right. "Jephro Rucastle.
SH-WWF17

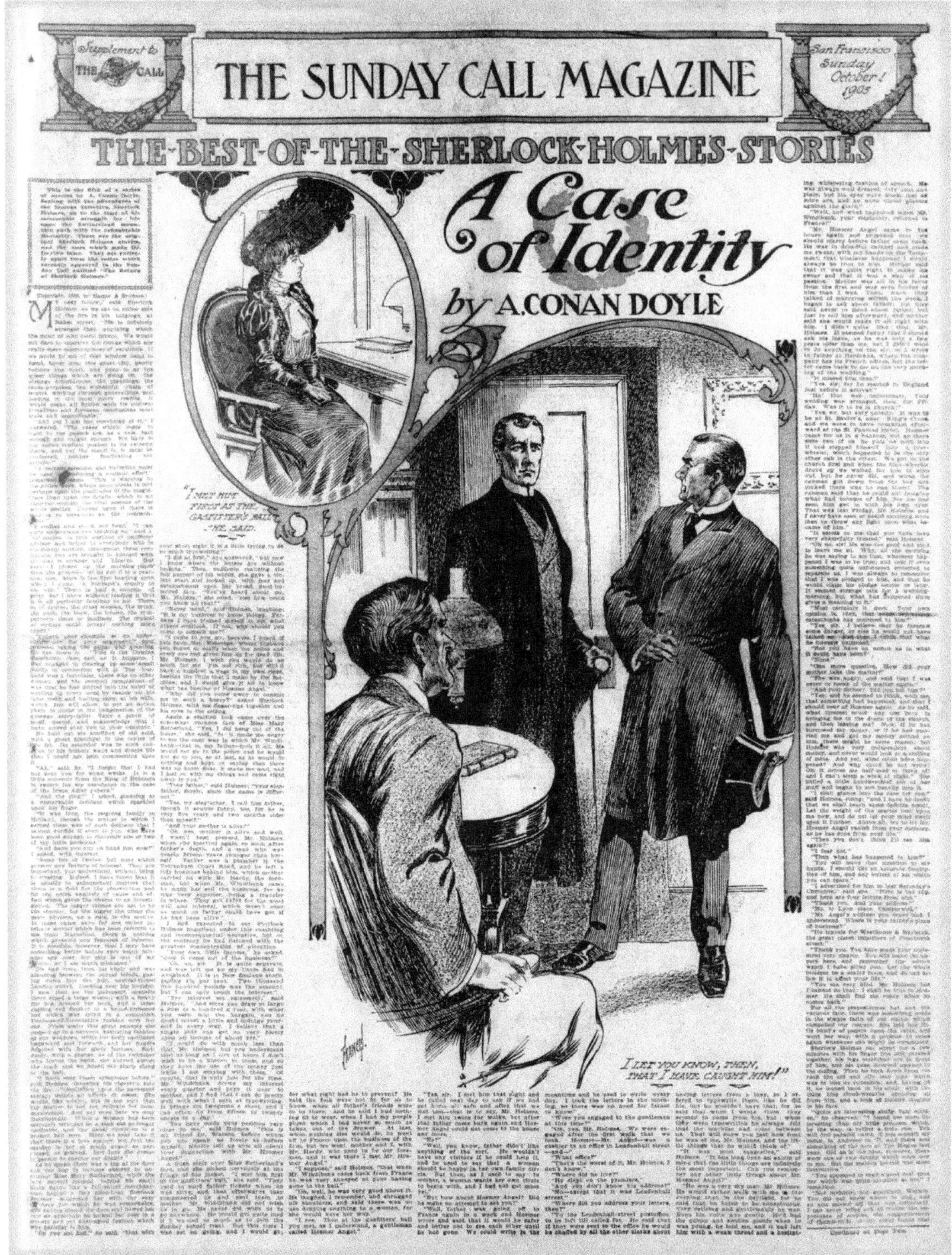

Supplement to THE CALL

THE SUNDAY CALL MAGAZINE

San Francisco Sunday October 1 1905

THE BEST OF THE SHERLOCK HOLMES STORIES

A Case of Identity

by A. CONAN DOYLE

Image 1/3. Front Page. "But the gentleman in the pew handed it up to her again."
SH-WWF18

Image 2/3. Front Page. "I met him first at the Gasfitter's ball," she said.
SH-WWF19

Image 3/3. Front Page. "I let you know, then, that I have caught him!"
SH-WWF20

Walter W. Francis - San Francisco Call:Red-Headed League, The 8th October 1905

Image 1/1. Front Page. In another instant he stood at the side of the hole, and was hauling up a companion
SH-WWF21

Image 1/1. Front Page. "But the gentleman in the pew handed it up to her again."
SH-WWF22

Supplement to THE CALL

THE SUNDAY CALL MAGAZINE

San Francisco Sunday October 22 1905

THE MYSTERY of Silver Blaze

BY A. CONAN DOYLE

INSIDE HUDDLED TOGETHER UPON A CHAIR HUNTER WAS SUNK IN A STATE OF ABSOLUTE STUPOR

AT THE BOTTOM OF THIS WAS FOUND THE DEAD BODY OF THE UNFORTUNATE TRAINER

Image 1/3. Front Page. "But the gentleman in the pew handed it up to her again." *SH-SEA20*

Stanley E. Armstrong - San Francisco Call:Silver Blaze 22nd October 1905

Image 2/3. Front Page at Top. Inside huddled together upon a chair. Hunter was sunk in a state of absolute stupor
SH-SEA21

Image 2/3. Front Page at Bottom. At the bottom of this was found the dead body of the unfortunate trainer.
SH-SEA22

Image 1/1. Front Page. "My God!" he cried, "what can be the meaning of this?"
SH-WWF23

Stanley E. Armstrong - San Francisco Call:Stockbroker's Clerk, The
5th November 1905

Image 1/1. Front Page. By that day you will be the business manager of the Franco-Midland Hardware Company, Limited.
SH-SEA23

Walter W. Francis - San Francisco Call:"Gloria Scott", The 12th November 1905

Image 1/1. Front Page. "We got on them before they could load?"
SH-WWF24

Stanley E. Armstrong - San Francisco Call:Musgrave Ritual, The 19th November 1905

Image 1/1. Front Page. It was the figure of a man with his forehead sunk on the edge of the box.
SH-SEA24

Joseph Clement Coll

Born 2nd July 1881 in Philadelphia
Died 19th October 1921

American newspaper and book illustrator who began his professional career working for the New York American before doing work for The North American, Collier's, Everybody's, and American Sunday Magazine. He illustrated many of Sir Arthur Conan Doyle's stories like, Sir Nigel (64) & The Lost World (46). He did one illustration that showed Sherlock Holmes as well as other characters from Doyle's stories.

Joseph Clement Coll – New York Tribune, The 6th September 1914

Image 1/2. Front Page. Featuring Sir Arthur Conan Doyle's stories, the Lost World, the story of Waterloo, Sir Nigel, The Refugees, The Last Galley, Micah Clarke. The Exploits of Brigadier Gerald and of course Sherlock Holmes, with a sign of four quote "Ah, Watson! In practice again," I observe. "How do you know?" "I see it, I deduce it, how do I know that you have been getting yourself very wet lately, and that you have a most clumsy and careless servant girl! Observations!"
SH-JCC1

Joseph Clement Coll – New York Tribune, The 6th September 1914

Image 2/2. "Ah, Watson! In practice again," I observe. "How do you know?" "I see it, I deduce it, how do I know that you have been getting yourself very wet lately, and that you have a most clumsy and careless servant girl! Observations!" The Sign of Four.
SH-JCC2

Pierre Georges Dutriac

Born 17th November 1866 in Bordeaux
Died 17th March 1958 in Charenton-le-Pont

French painter and illustrator who was active from 1902 to 1942. He illustrated many French novels including those by Émile Driant, Gaston Chérau and Jules Verne.

He illustrated 20 images for the Sherlock Holmes stories.

Date	French Title	English Title	Images	Publication
Oct 1921	Le Pied du diable 1	The Adventure of the Devil's Foot 1	3	Lectures Pour Tous
Nov 1921	Le Pied du diable 2	The Adventure of the Devil's Foot 2	3	Lectures Pour Tous
16th Dec 1923	Sherlock Holmes mourant	The Adventure of the Dying Detective	2	Excelsior Dimanche
20th Nov 1927	La Boite de Carton	The Adventure of the Cardboard Box	1	Dimanche Illustré
2nd Sep 1928	Vampire, La	The Adventure of the Sussex Vampire	2	Dimanche Illustré
14th Oct 1928	Les Plans du Bruce Partington	The Adventure of Bruce Partington Plans	1	Dimanche Illustré
2nd Jun 1929	Le Mystère de Wisteria Lodge	The Adventure of Wisteria Lodge	1	Dimanche Illustré
1st Dec 1929	Le Chatelain de Shoscombe	The Adventure of Shoscombe Old Place	1	Dimanche Illustré
5th Jan 1930	Le Diamant Jaune	The Adventure of the Mazarin Stone	1	Dimanche Illustré
30th Mar 1930	Les trois Garrideb	The Adventure of the Three Garridebs	1	Dimanche Illustré
10th Aug 1930	L'Homme qui Rampe	The Adventure of the Creeping Man	1	Dimanche Illustré
25th Jan 1931	Le Mystère du Pont de Thor	The Adventure of Thor Bridge	1	Dimanche Illustré
22nd Feb 1931	Le Criniere de Lion	The Adventure of the Lion's Mane	2	Dimanche Illustré

Pierre Georges Dutriac - Le Pied du diable (The Adventure of the Devil's Foot)
(October 1921, Lectures Pour Tous)

Image 1/6. Page 81. Sherlock Holmes in deep thought with his pipe.
SH-PGD1

Pierre Georges Dutriac - Le Pied du diable (The Adventure of the Devil's Foot) (October 1921, Lectures Pour Tous

Image 2/6. Page 83. Owen and George Tregennis being taken away.
SH-PGD2

Pierre Georges Dutriac - Le Pied du diable (The Adventure of the Devil's Foot) (October 1921, Lectures Pour Tous

Image 3/6. Page 85. Brenda Tregennis dead in our chair.
SH-PGD3

Pierre Georges Dutriac - Le Pied du diable (The Adventure of the Devil's Foot) (November 1921, Lectures Pour Tous)

Image 4/6. Page 257. Title for the November's issue.
SH-PGD4

Pierre Georges Dutriac - Le Pied du diable (The Adventure of the Devil's Foot) (November 1921, Lectures Pour Tous

Ah! tenez, le voici, un peu en avance. Vous plairait-il de venir de ce côté, docteur Sterndale ? Nous avons fait tantôt dans la maison une expérience de chimie qui ne nous permet guère d'y recevoir un visiteur aussi distingué que vous. »

Image 5/6. Page 261. (Ah! here it is, a little early. Would you like to come this way, Doctor Sterndale? We have done sometimes in the House an experience of chemistry which hardly allows us to receive a visitor as distinguished as you.)
SH-PGD5

Pierre Georges Dutriac - Le Pied du diable (The Adventure of the Devil's Foot) (November 1921, Lectures Pour Tous

Image 6/6. Page 264. Mortimer Tregennis dead like his sister Brenda.
SH-PGD6

Pierre Georges Dutriac – Sherlock Holmes mourant (The Adventure of the Dying Detective) (16th December 1923, Excelsior Dimanche)

C'était un charmant objet, que j'allais prendre pour l'examiner de près, quand Holmes poussa un cri terrible, un hurlement qu'on dût entendre de la rue. Je me retournai : je vis une figure convulsée et des yeux hagards.

Image 1/2. Page 6. (It was a charming object, which had to be picked up to examine it closely, when Holmes let up a terrible cry, a howl that was said to have been heard in the street.)
SH-PGD7

Pierre Georges Dutriac – Sherlock Holmes mourant (The Adventure of the Dying Detective) (16th December 1923, Excelsior Dimanche

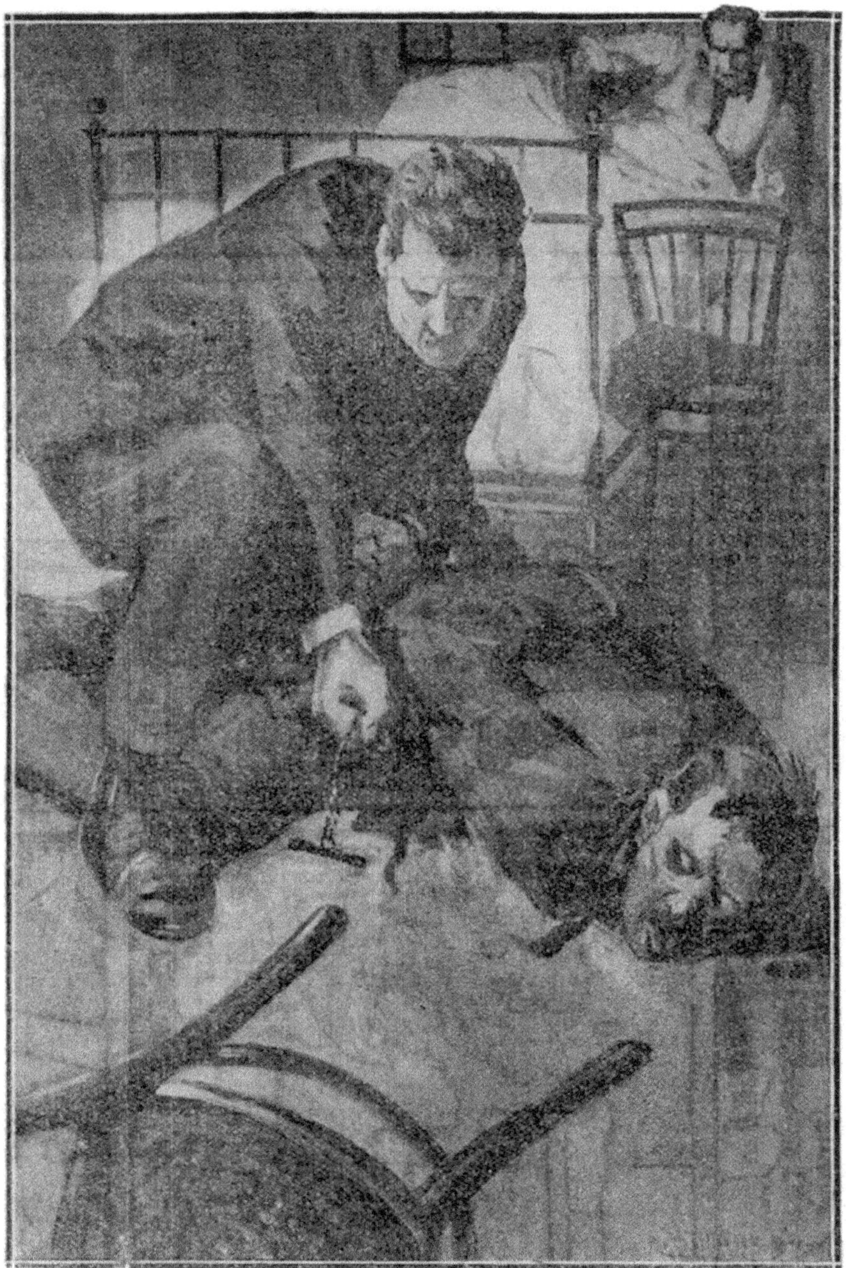

Mais alors j'entendis le bruit d'un bond, que suivit le bruit d'une lutte; puis un tintement de métal, puis un cri de douleur. "Vous ne réussirez qu'à vous faire du mal, dit l'inspecteur. Voulez-vous rester tranquille?"

Image 2/2. Page 7. (But then I heard the sound of a leap, followed by the sound of a struggle: then a tinkling of metal, a cry of pain.
"You will only succeed in hurting yourself," said the teacher. "Do you want to keep quiet?)
SH-PGD8

Pierre Georges Dutriac – Boite de Carton, La (The Adventure of the Cardboard Box)
(20th November 1927, Dimanche Illustré)

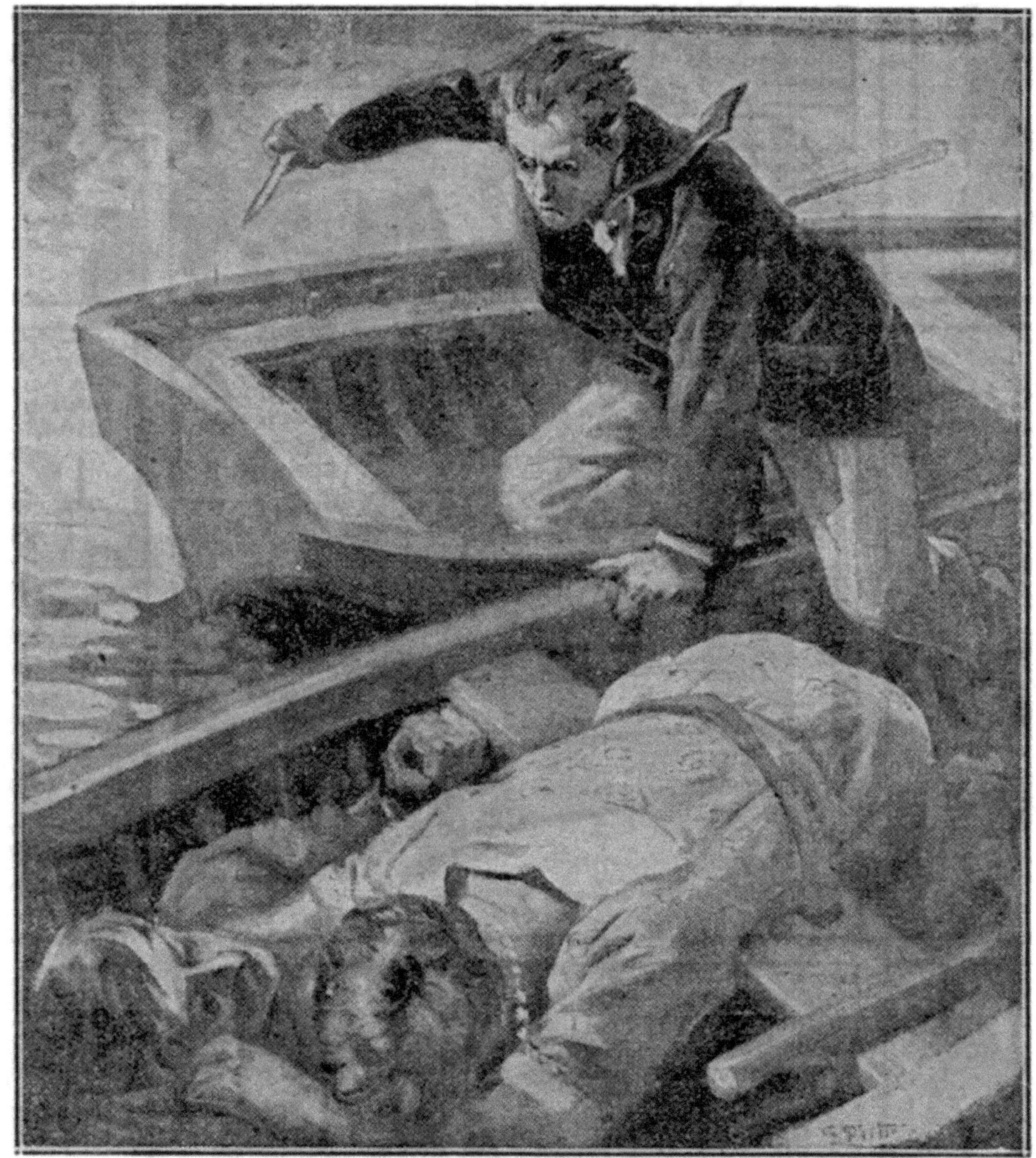

Elle, je l'aurais épargnée peut-être, malgré sa folie ; mais elle l'entoura de ses bras, pleurant et l'appelant Alec. Je frappai de nouveau et l'étendis à son côté.

Image 1/1. Page 7. (I would have spared her, perhaps, for all my madness, but she threw her arms round him, crying out to him, and calling him "Alec." I struck again, and she lay stretched beside him.)
SH-PGD9

Pierre Georges Dutriac – Vampire, La (The Adventure of the Sussex Vampire) 2nd September 1928, Dimanche Illustré

Au moment où la nourrice se précipitait dans la chambre, elle vit sa maîtresse penchée sur le bébé, comme pour lui mordre le cou. Et le fait est qu'il portait une blessure d'où le sang jaillissait.

Image 1/2. Page 6. (As the nurse rushed into the hallway, she saw her mistress leaning over the baby.
as if to bite his neck. And the fact is that he had a wound from which blood was gushing.
SH-PGD10

Pierre Georges Dutriac – Vampire, La (The Adventure of the Sussex Vampire) 2nd September 1928, Dimanche Illustré)

Un épagneul venait de se lever et, lentement, s'avançait vers son maître. Il marchait avec peine ; son train d'arrière se mouvait d'une façon irrégulière, sa queue traînait sur le sol.

Image 2/2. Page 7. (A spaniel had lain in a basket in the corner. It came slowly forward towards its master, walking with difficulty. Its hind legs moved irregularly, and its tail was on the ground.)
SH-PGD11

Pierre Georges Dutriac – Plans du Bruce Partington, Les (The Adventure of Bruce Partington Plans) 14th October 1928, Dimanche Illustré)

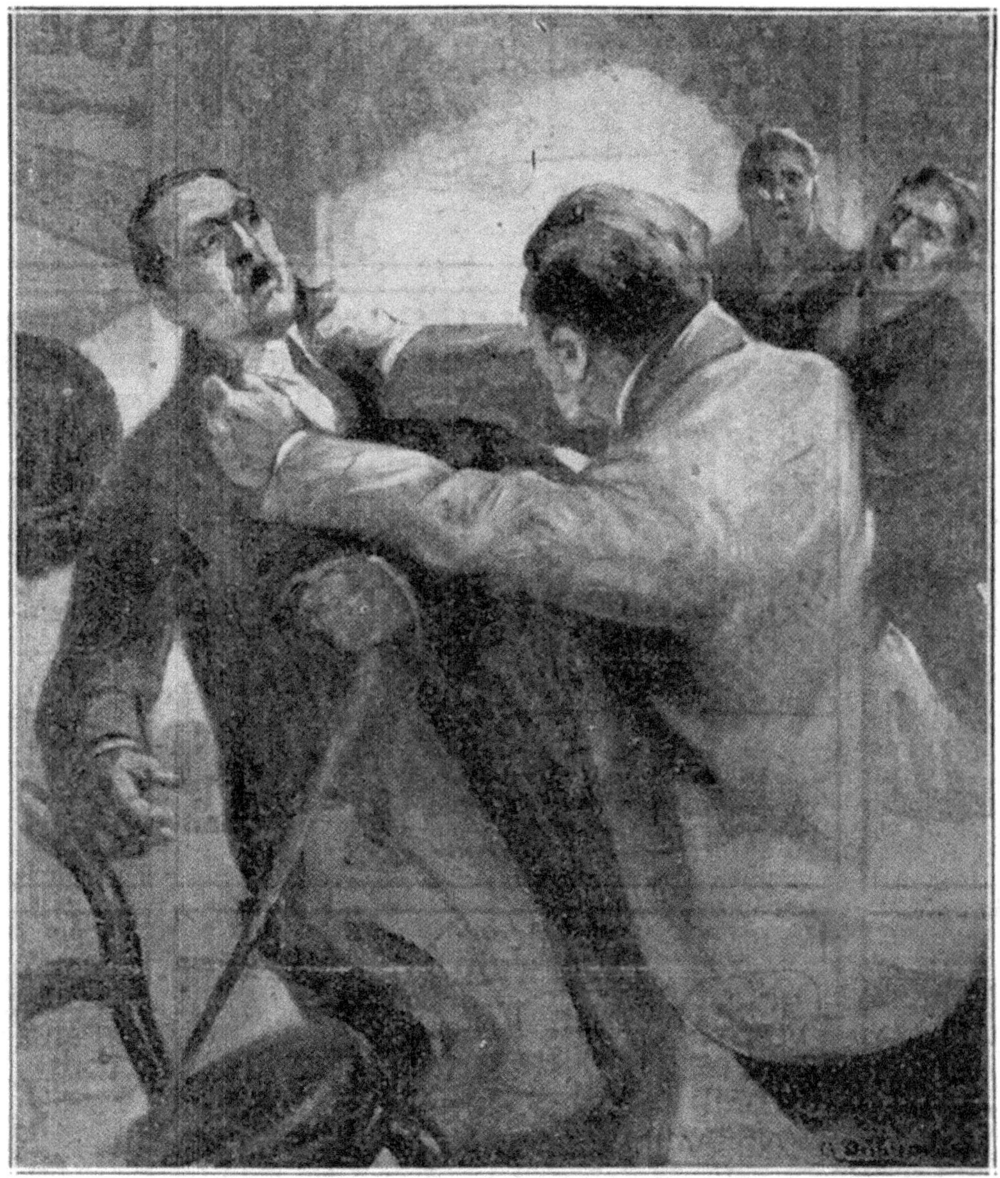

Le visiteur apparut devant nous. Il voulut fuir ; Holmes l'empoigna au collet. Il promena autour de lui des yeux hagards, chancela, tomba sans connaissance. Son chapeau roula sur le parquet.

Image 1/1. Page 7. (Our visitor stood before us. Holmes caught him by the collar. The man glared round him, staggered, and fell senseless upon the floor. With the shock, his broad-brimmed hat flew from his head.
SH-PGD12

Pierre Georges Dutriac – Le Mystère de Wisteria Lodge, (The Adventure of Wisteria Lodge) 2nd June 1929, Dimanche Illustré)

« *En ce qui concerne Garcia, dit Gregson, on l'a trouvé mort, ce matin, sur un terrain vague.* »

Image 1/1. Page 7. ("As to Garcia," said Gregson, "he was found dead this morning upon Oxshott Common.")
SH-PGD13

Pierre Georges Dutriac – Chatelain de Shoscombe, Le (The Adventure of Shoscombe Old Place) 1st December 1929, Dimanche Illustré)

Un homme s'encadra dans l'ogive de la voûte. Il était véritablement terrible à voir. Une grande lanterne d'écurie qu'il portait à longueur de bras, éclairait son visage.

Image 1/1. Page 7. (A man appeared in the Gothic archway. He was a terrible figure, huge in stature and fierce in manner.)
SH-PGD14

Pierre Georges Dutriac – Le Diamant Jaune (The Adventure of the Mazarin Stone) 5th January 1930, Dimanche Illustré)

*Il se ramassait sur lui-même, prêt à bondir, quand la porte de la chambre à coucher s'étant ouverte, une voix se fit entendre, glaciale et sardonique : « **Hé là, comte ! Vous n'allez pas m'abîmer ça ?** »*

Image 2/2. Page 7. (He was crouching for his final spring and blow when a cool, sardonic voice greeted him from the open bedroom door: "Don't break it, Count! Don't break it!".) *SH-PGD15*

Pierre Georges Dutriac – Les trois Garrideb (The Adventure of the Three Garridebs) 30th March 1930, Dimanche Illustré)

Une figure inquiète avait surgi soudain de l'ouverture, avec une expression de dépit et de rage, qui fit place à une grimace de confusion devant la menace de nos deux revolvers braqués.

Image 1/1. Page 7. (A worried face had suddenly appeared from the opening, with the expression of annoyance that gave way to a grimace of confusion at the treat of our two-pointed revolvers.)
SH-PGD16

Pierre Georges Dutriac – L'Homme qui Rampe (The Adventure of the Creeping Man)
10th August 1930, Dimanche Illustré)

L'homme et le chien roulèrent ensembre sur le sol, l'un poussant des grognements terribles.

Image 1/1. Page 7. (The man and the dog rolled together on the ground, one uttering terrible grunts.)
SH-PGD17

Pierre Georges Dutriac – Le Mystère du Pont de Thor (The Adventure of Thor Bridge) 25th January 1931, Dimanche Illustré)

« Je m'enfuis en me bouchant les oreilles. Elle était, dans ce moment, à l'entrée du pont, d'où elle vomissait contre moi les imprécations et les invectives ».

Image 1/1. Page 7. ("I put my hands to my ears and rushed away. When I left her, she was standing still shrieking out her curses at me, in the mouth of the bridge.")
SH-PGD18

Pierre Georges Dutriac – Le Criniere de Lion (The Adventure of the Lion's Mane) 22nd February 1931, Dimanche Illustré)

Soudain, levant les bras, il poussa un cri terrible et s'abattit, la face contre terre. Stackhurst et moi, nous nous élançâmes : Fitzroy McPherson se mourait.

Image 1/2. Page 6. (Suddenly, raising his arms, he uttered a terrible cry and collapsed, his face against earth. Stackhurst and I rushed in: Fitzroy McPherson was dying.)
SH-PGD19

Pierre Georges Dutriac – Le Criniere de Lion (The Adventure of the Lion's Mane)
22nd February 1931, Dimanche Illustré

— Je me promenais en haut des falaises, quand j'entendis ses cris. Il était au bord de l'eau. Je descendis au pas de course et l'aidai à remonter.

Image 2/2. Page 7. (I was walking on top of the cliffs when I heard his cries. It was at the water's edge. I ran down and helped him back up.)
SH-PGD20

B. Widman

B. Widman was an American illustrator and I have completely failed to find out his first name or any other biographical information about him, maybe in future editions, more information will be forthcoming, until then.
In 1902, he did 13 illustrations for Arthur Conan Doyle's Story The Hound of the Baskervilles, which were printed in The St. Louis Republic over the 13 weeks from 13th July to the 5th October 1902
Most of his illustrations are acknowledged replicas of Sidney Paget illustrations. Widman signed some with "B. Widman after S. Paget" or "B. Widman S. P." in honour of Paget.

B. Widman - The Hound of the Baskervilles - The St. Louis Republic, The 13th July 1902

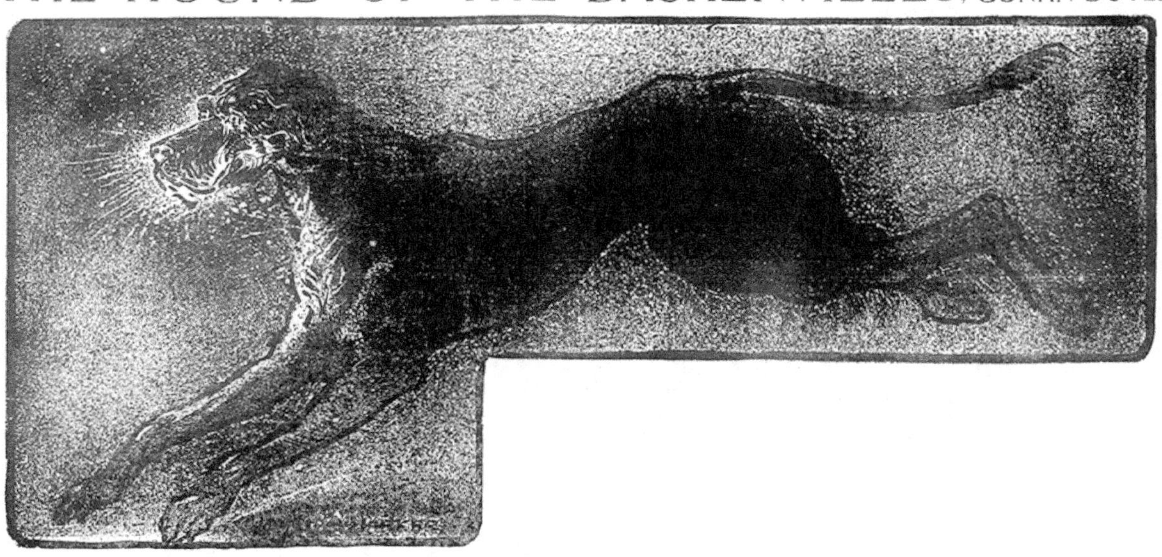

Image 1/13. Page 40.
SH-BW1

B. Widman - The Hound of the Baskervilles - The St. Louis Republic, The 20th July 1902

I WAS AWARE OF A BUSHY BLACK BEARD AND A PAIR OF PIERCING BLACK EYES TURNED UPON US.

Image 2/13. Page 40. I was aware of a bushy black beard and a pair of piercing black eyes turned upon us.
SH-BW2

B. Widman - The Hound of the Baskervilles - The St. Louis Republic, The 27th July 1902

THE DRIVER POINTED WITH HIS WHIP. "BASKERVILLE HALL," SAID HE.

Image 3/13. Page 43.
SH-BW3

B. Widman - The Hound of the Baskervilles - The St. Louis Republic, The 3rd August 1902

HIS FACE SEEMED TO BE RIGID WITH EXPECTATION AS HE STARED OUT INTO THE BLACKNESS OF THE MOOR.

Image 4/13. Page 43.
SH-BW4

B. Widman - The Hound of the Baskervilles - The St. Louis Republic, The 10th August 1902

SIR HENRY SUDDENLY DREW MISS STAPLETON TO HIS SIDE.

Image 5/13. Page 43. Sir Henry suddenly drew Miss Stapleton to his side.
SH-BW5

B. Widman - The Hound of the Baskervilles - The St. Louis Republic, The 17th August 1902

"THERE'S FOUL PLAY SOMEWHERE AND THERE'S BLACK VILLAINY BREWING!"

Image 6/13. Page 43.
SH-BW6

B. Widman - The Hound of the Baskervilles - The St. Louis Republic, The 24th August 1902

"IT WAS ABOUT THE LATE SIR CHARLES BASKERVILLE THAT I HAVE COME HERE TO SEE YOU."

Image 7/13. Page 43. "It was about the late Sir Charles Baskerville that I have come here to see you."
SH-BW7

B. Widman - The Hound of the Baskervilles - The St. Louis Republic, The 31st August 1902

I SHRANK BACK INTO THE DARKEST CORNER, AND COCKED THE PISTOL IN MY POCKET.

Image 8/13. Page 40. I shrank back into the darkest corner and cocked the pistol in my pocket.
SH-BW8

B. Widman - The Hound of the Baskervilles - The St. Louis Republic, The 7th September 1902

IT WAS A PROSTRATE MAN, FACE DOWNWARDS.

Image 9/13. Page 52. It was a prostrate man, face downwards.
SH-BW9

B. Widman - The Hound of the Baskervilles - The St. Louis Republic, The 14th September 1902

THE MOON SHONE UPON HIM, AND I COULD DISTINGUISH THE DAPPER SHAPE AND JAUNTY WALK OF THE NATURALIST.

Image 10/13. Page 37. The moon shone upon him, and I could distinguish the dapper shape and jaunty walk of the naturalist.
SH-BW10

B. Widman - The Hound of the Baskervilles - The St. Louis Republic, The 21st September 1902

HE STOOD UPON A CHAIR AND CURVED HIS RIGHT ARM OVER THE BROAD HAT AND ROUND THE LONG RINGLETS.

Image 11/13. Page 54. He stood upon a chair and curved his right arm over the broad hat and round the long ringlets.
SH-BW11

B. Widman - The Hound of the Baskervilles - The St. Louis Republic, The 28th September 1902

I was in time to see the beast spring upon his victim, hurl him to the ground.

Image 12/13. Page 54. I was in time to see the beast spring upon his victim, hurl him to the ground.
SH-BW12

B. Widman - The Hound of the Baskervilles - The St. Louis Republic, The 5th October 1902

"AND NOW, MY DEAR WATSON, WE HAVE HAD SOME WEEKS OF SEVERE WORK, AND FOR ONE EVENING, I THINK, WE MAY TURN OUR THOUGHTS INTO MORE PLEASANT CHANNELS."

Image 13/13. Page 56. "And now, my dear Watson, we have had some weeks of severe work and for one evening, I think, we may turn our thoughts into more pleasant channels."
SH-BW13

Paul Henri Thiriat

Born 30th December 1868 in Paris
Died 11th April 1943 in Paris

Started life as an engraver using the name Henri Thiriat for l 'illustration in 1890 and Le Tour du monde in 1892. After 1896 he devoted himself to watercolours and drawing. He did a number of covers for a number of French publications including Le Petit Journal and Mon Bonheur, for which publication he did 16 illustrations for the Hound of the Baskervilles. After World War l, he continued his activity as a press illustrator signing as Whip or Thiriat for various publications including L 'Aventure, where he illustrated the Lion's Mane, the Blanched soldier, Boscombe Valley mystery and the blanched Colourman.

Thiriat, Paul Henri - Le Chien des Baskervilles – Mon Bonheur 31st January 1907

La lune éclairait faiblement l'étroite vallée... Au milieu, la pauvre jeune fille gisiat inanimée, à l'endroit où elle était tombée, morte de fatigue ou de peur... Ce qui effraya le plus les trois sacripants, ce fut une horrible bête qui tenait ses crocs enfoncés dans la gorge de Hugo. Au moment où ils s'approchaient, elle arracha un lambeau de chair du cou de Baskerville et tourna vers eux ses prunelles de feu et sa gueule rouge de sang.

Image 1/13. Page 131. (The moon was faintly lighting up the narrow valley...in the middle, the poor young girl lay motionless, at the spot where she had fallen, dead of fatigue or of fear...what frightened the three scoundrels the most was a horrible beast that had its fangs sunk in Hugo's throat. as they approached, it tore a shred of flesh from Baskerville's neck and turned her eyes of fire and her blood-red face towards them.)

SH-PHT1

Thiriat, Paul Henri - Le Chien des Baskervilles – Mon Bonheur, The 7th February 1907

« J'examinai attentivement le cadavre, auquel on n'avait pas encore touché. Sir Charles était étendu, la face contre terre, les bras en croix, les doigts crispés dans le sol... »

Image 2/13. Page 189. (I carefully examined the corpse, which had not yet been touched. Sir Charles was stretched out, face down, arms outstretched, fingers clenched in the ground...)

SH-PHT2

Thiriat, Paul Henri - Le Chien des Baskervilles – Mon Bonheur, The 14th February 1907

Je vis un hansom-cab, *rangé le long du trottoir, reprendre sa marche en avant. Un voyageur l'occupait.*
« – Voilà notre homme! s'écria Holmes. Venez vite! Nous pourrons au moins le dévisager faute de mieux! » Comme dans un éclair, je vis une barbe noire broussailleuse et des yeux perçants qui nous regardaient à travers la glace du cab.

Image 3/13. Page 197. (saw him in a hansom-cab, parked along the sidewalk, resumed his march forward. A traveller occupied it.
'Here is our man!' cried Holmes. 'Come quickly! As if in a flash, I saw a bushy black beard and piercing eyes watching us through the cab window.)
SH-PHT3

Thiriat, Paul Henri - Le Chien des Baskervilles – Mon Bonheur, The 21st February 1907

— J'ai reçu du bureau central un message m'avertissant que, dans cette maison, un bourgeois avait pris des renseignements sur le 2.704... J'arrive tout droit de la remise pour que vous m'expliquiez ce que vous avez contre moi... »

Image 4/13. Page 253. (I received a message from the central office warning me that in this house. a bourgeois had taken information on the 2,704... I have arrived now, so that you explain to me what you have against me...")
SH-PHT4

Thiriat, Paul Henri - Le Chien des Baskervilles – Mon Bonheur, The 28th February 1907

A la clarté pâlissante de ce soir d'automne, je vis que le centre du château était formé par une construction massive. La façade disparaissait sous les lierres... « — Soyez le bienvenu au château de Baskerville, sir Henry, » dit une voix. Un homme de haute taille s'était avancé....

Image 5/13. Page 279. (In the fading light of this autumn evening, I saw that the centre of the castle was formed by a massive construction. The facade disappeared under the ivy... "Welcome to Baskerville Castle, Sir Henry," said a voice. A tall man came forward....)
SH-PHT5

Thiriat, Paul Henri - Le Chien des Baskervilles – Mon Bonheur, The 7th March 1907

En étouffant le bruit de mes pas, je me glissai le long du passage et j'avançai ma tête par l'ouverture de la porte. Barrymore était blotti dans le coin de la fenêtre, sa bougie tout près de la vitre.

Image 6/13. Page 293. (Muffling the sound of my footsteps, I slipped down the passage and stuck my head through the opening of the door. Barrymore was huddled in the corner of the window, his candle close to the glass.)
SH-PHT6

Thiriat, Paul Henri - Le Chien des Baskervilles – Mon Bonheur, The 14th March 1907

« Non monsieur... non, vas contre vous, » fit une voix de femme. Nous nous retournâmes, et, nous aperçumes Mme Barrymore, plus pâle et plus terrifiée que son mari.

Image 7/13. Page 349. ("No sir...no, not against you," said a woman's voice. We turned round, and saw Mrs. Barrymore, paler and more terrified than her husband.)
SH-PHT7

Thiriat, Paul Henri - Le Chien des Baskervilles – Mon Bonheur, The 21st March 1907

Parvenus au sommet du monticule, nous distinguâmes Selden qui descendait précipitamment la pente escarpée...

Image 8/13. Page 363. ("When we reached the top of the mound, we could make out Selden descending hurriedly up the steep slope...)
SH-PHT8

Thiriat, Paul Henri - Le Chien des Baskervilles – Mon Bonheur, The 28th March 1907

Je gravis le Pic Noir, et du haut de sa cime rocheuse, je contemplai la plaine dénudée qui s'étendait à mes pieds.

Image 9/13. Page 389. ("I climbed the black peak, and from the top of its rocky summit, I contemplated the denuded plain which stretched out at my feet.)
SH-PHT9

Thiriat, Paul Henri - Le Chien des Baskervilles – Mon Bonheur, The 4th April 1907

J'armai mon revolver, déterminé à ne me montrer qu'au moment où l'inconnu pénétrerait dans la hutte... Les pas se rapprochèrent encore... Une ombre se dessina dans l'encadrement de la porte...

Image 10/13. Page 445. (I cocked my revolver, determined not to show myself until the stranger entered the hut... The footsteps came closer still... A shadow appeared in the doorway...)
SH-PHT10

Thiriat, Paul Henri - Le Chien des Baskervilles – Mon Bonheur, The 11th April 1907

Nous redescendîmes dans la salle à manger, et, là, son bougeoir à la main, il attira mon attention sur la vieille peinture que le temps avait recouverte de sa patine. « — Ressemble-t-il à quelqu'un que vous connaissiez ?» me demanda Sherlock Holmes.

Image 11/13. Page 459. (We went back down to the dining room, and there, his candlestick in his hand, he drew my attention to the old painting that time had salvaged from its patina. "Does he look like someone you know?" Sherlock Holmes asks me.)
SH-PHT11

Thiriat, Paul Henri - Le Chien des Baskervilles – Mon Bonheur, The 18th April 1907

Une effroyable apparition venait de surgir des profondeurs du brouillard. C'était un chien! un énorme chien noir... Sa gueule soufflait du feu; ses prunelles luisaient comme des charbons ardents; autour de ses babines et de ses crocs vacillaient des flammes.

Image 12/13. Page 485. (A frightful apparition had just emerged from the depths of the fog. It was a dog! an enormous black dog... Its mouth blew fire; his eyes shone like hot coals; around his chops and his fangs flickered flames.)
SH-PHT12

Thiriat, Paul Henri - Le Chien des Baskervilles – Mon Bonheur, The 25th April 1907

Une niche et un amas d'os indiquaient l'endroit où Stapleton attachait son chien. Un crâne auquel adhéraient encore des poils noirs, gisait au milieu des débris.

Image 13/13. Page 521. (A niche in a heap of bones indicating! the place where Stapleton tied up his dog. An unidentified skull, still adhering black hairs, lay amidst the debris.)
SH-PHT13

Thiriat, Paul Henri - le-mystere-de-la-vallee-de-boscombe – Mon Bonheur, The 28th November 1907

Sur ses indications, on trouva le cadavre de son père étendu sur l'herbe, près de l'étang...

Image 1/3. Page 675. (On his directions, they found his father's dead body lying on the grass, near the pond...)
SH-PHT14

Thiriat, Paul Henri - Le Chien des Baskervilles – Mon Bonheur, The 5th December 1907

La porte s'ouvrit et donna passage à la plus ravissante jeune fille que j'aie jamais vue: ses yeux avaient un éclat tout particulier; ses lèvres étaient d'un dessin très pur. Elle avait enfin ce naturel parfait que lui donnait l'oubli complet d'elle-même devant la seule pensée et la grande préoccupation qui la dominaient.

Image 2/3. Page 731. (The door opened and gave passage to the most ravishing young girl I had ever seen in my life; her eyes had a peculiar sparkle; her lips underpinned with a very pure design. Finally, she had that perfect naturalness that gave her a complete oblivion of herself in front of the only thought and the great preoccupation which dominated her)

SH-PHT15

Thiriat, Paul Henri - Le Chien des Baskervilles – Mon Bonheur, The 12th December 1907

« — M. John Turner! » annonça le garçon d'hôtel en ouvrant la porte de notre salon et en introduisant un visiteur. L'homme qui entra avait une tournure étrange et bien faite pour impressionner. Il était boiteux, et ses épaules voûtées le faisaient paraître plus âgé qu'il n'était réellement. Ses traits durs, accentués, et ses membres robustes dénotaient une force physique et morale peu ordinaire. Sa barbe embroussaillée, ses cheveux grisonnants, ses épais sourcils retombant sur ses yeux se combinaient pour donner à sa personne un aspect d'énergie.

Image 3/3. Page 759. ("Mr. John Turner!" announced the waiter by opening the door of our living room by introducing a visitor. The man who entered had a strange and well made to impress. He was lame, and his hunched shoulders made him look older than he really was. His hard, accentuated features and sturdy limbs denoted unusual physical and moral strength. His bushy beard, his greying hair, his thick eyebrows falling over his eyes combined to give his person an aspect of energy.)
SH-PHT16

Thiriat, Paul Henri – Un Pauvre Vieux – L'Aventure, The 28th July 1927

Image 1/2. Page 28. Story Title - A poor old man, (the retired Colourman)
SH-PHT17

Thiriat, Paul Henri – Un Pauvre Vieux – L'Aventure, The 28th July 1927

— **Qu'avez-vous fait des cadavres ?**

Image 2/2. Page 11. What did you do with the corpses?)
SH-PHT18

Thiriat, Paul Henri – Le Soldat Decolore – L'Aventure, The 22nd September 1927

Image 1/3. Page 11. Title Page – The discoloured Soldier (The Blanched Soldier)
SH-PHT19

- Par ici, monsieur ! m'ordonna-t-il à voix basse.

Image 2/3. Page 12. Over here, Sir! He ordered in a low voice.
SH-PHT20

Thiriat, Paul Henri – Le Soldat Decolore – L'Aventure, The 22nd September 1927

Jne sorte de nabot, à tête bulbeuse, jacassait en hollandais, l'air très exalté.

Image 3/3. Page 13. One kind of dwarf, with a bulbous head, chattered in Dutch, looking very excited.
SH-PHT21

Henry Matthew Brock

Born 11th July 1875 in Cambridge (UK)
Died 21st July 1960 in the Evelyn Nursing Home, Cambridge

Brock was a British illustrator and landscape painter.
One of four sons of Edmund Brock and his wife Mary Ann Louise. He was the younger brother of the better-known artist Charles Edmund Brock. He studied at the Cambridge School of Art. His brother painted in oils and was elected a member of the British Institution, while he worked made illustrates for the magazine Punch as well as books.

In March and April 1911, he and Joseph William Simpson shared the illustrations for The Red Circle, which appeared in the Strand Magazine. These illustrations don't have signatures, but it is likely that the following 6 images are Brock. The first image clearly shows Sidney Paget images around.

Henry Matthew Brock – The Red Circle – The Strand, March 1911

" HOLMES STARED WITH GREAT CURIOSITY AT THE SLIPS OF FOOLSCAP."

Image 1/6. Page 261. "Holmes stared with great curiosity at the slips of foolscap."
SH-HMB1

"THEY BUNDLED HIM INTO A CAB THAT WAS BESIDE THE KERB."

Image 2/6. Page 263. "They bundled him into a cab that was beside the kerb."
SH-HMB2

Henry Matthew Brock – The Red Circle – The Strand, March 1911

"I CAUGHT A GLIMPSE OF A DARK, BEAUTIFUL, HORRIFIED FACE GLARING AT THE NARROW OPENING OF THE BOX-ROOM

Vol. xli.—34.

Image 3/6. Page 265. "I caught a glimpse of a dark, beautiful, horrified face glaring at the narrow opening of the box room."
SH-HMB3

Henry Matthew Brock – The Red Circle – The Strand, April 1911

"HOLMES WAS PASSING THE CANDLE BACKWARDS AND FORWARDS ACROSS THE WINDOW-PANES."

Image 4/6. Page 429. "Holmes was passing the candle backwards and forwards across the window-Panes."
SH-HMB4

Henry Matthew Brock – The Red Circle – The Strand, April 1911

"'BY GEORGE! IT'S BLACK GORGIANO HIMSELF!' CRIED THE AMERICAN DETECTIVE."

Image 5/6. Page 431 " ' by George! It's Black Gorgiano himself!' cried the American detective."
SH-HMB5

Henry Matthew Brock – The Red Circle – The Strand, April 1911

"SLOWLY SHE ADVANCED, HER FACE PALE AND DRAWN WITH A FRIGHTFUL APPREHENSION."

Image 6/6. Page 433 " Slowly she advanced. Her face pale and drawn with a frightful apprehension."
SH-HMB6

Joseph William Simpson

Born 1878 in Carlisle, Cumberland
Died 1939 in London

British Painter and etcher of portraits and sporting subjects, he was also a magazine illustrator.
He did one Sherlock Holmes picture featuring 12 of Sidney Paget's Sherlock Holmes images.
From Top Left to Bottom Right

- The Second Stain (Paget's last sherlock Holmes Story)
- The Solitary Cyclist
- The Dancing Men
- The Hound of the Baskervilles
- The Speckled Band
- The Reigate Squire
- The Boscombe Valley Mystery
- The Red-Headed League
- The Norwood Builder
- The Abbey Grange
- The Final Problem
- The Bruce Partington Plans

Joseph William Simpson– The Red Circle – The Strand, March 1911

A REVERIE.

Image 1/1. Page 258. A Reverie.
SH-JWS1

Born 4th July 1867 New York

Died 2nd December 1924 Riverdale New York

American painter and illustrator. In 1890 he travelled to Munich, Germany to study under Ludwig von Loeffiz. He returned After two years of study. Before leaving Munich, Keller received the Hallgarten Prize, and his painting "At Mass" was purchased by the Academy, it was later destroyed during an Allied bombing raid in WW II. The arts critic Walter Jack Duncan wrote: "Keller, was a born artist. By instinct we recognize this at once. His simplest sketch, every stroke of his brush or pencil, is nervous with artistic energy. One feels it pulsating sturdily through all his multifarious work, through his graceful and sinuous drawings, his exquisite watercolours, his crowded and animated oils. His preliminary sketches especially, so fluent, natural, unaffected, flowing straight out of his facile pencil and confessing all it is possible to know of an artist's talent, prove beyond question that here was a man who was an artist in the full meaning of the word; as the actors used to say, *an artist to the fingertips*."

Keller produced 11 illustrations for the New York Tribune from 20th September 1914 until 22nd November 1914, the quality isn't wonderful because the images were printed on newspaper, and in many cases the image was split over a couple of pages, they have been re-joined.

Arthur Ignatius Keller – The Valley of Fear – The New-York Tribune, 20th September 1914

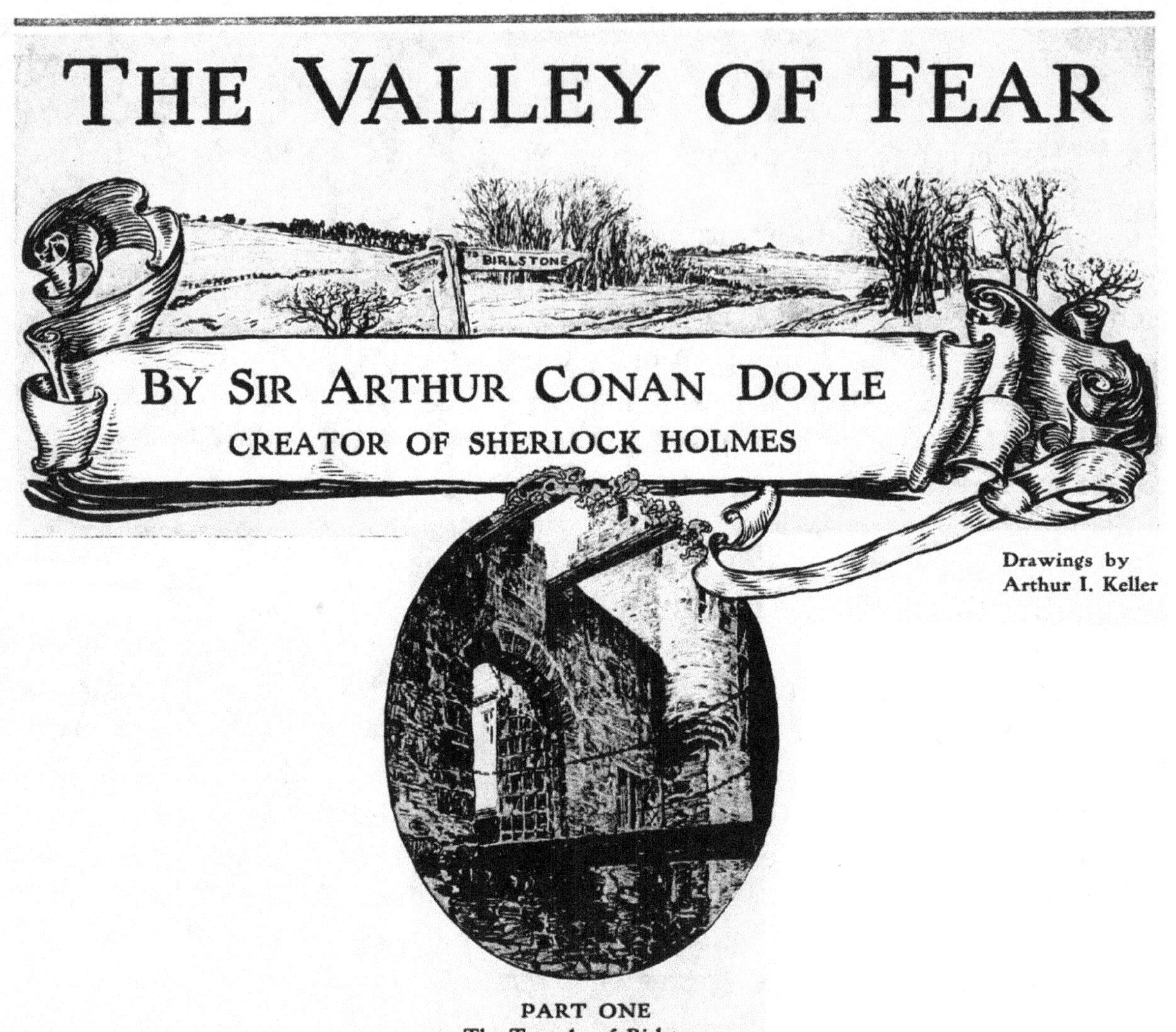

Image 1/11. Page 3. Title.
SH-AIK1

Arthur Ignatius Keller – The Valley of Fear – The New-York Tribune, 20th September 1914

"What's this, Mr. Holmes? Man, it's witchcraft! Where in the name of all that's wonderful did you get those names?"

Image 2/11. Page 5. "What's this, Mr. Holmes? Man, it's witchcraft! Where in the name of all that's wonderful did you get those names?"
SH-AIK2

Arthur Ignatius Keller – The Valley of Fear – The New-York Tribune, 27th September 1914

Image 3/11. Page 10-11. "I understand that you have often seen this very unusual mark upon Mr. Douglas' forearm?"
SH-AIK3

Arthur Ignatius Keller – The Valley of Fear – The New-York Tribune, 27th September 1914

FOR AN INSTANT I COULD HAVE SWORN THAT THE FAINTEST SHADOW OF A SMILE FLICKERED OVER THE WOMAN'S LIPS.

Image 4/11. Page 10-11. For an instant I could have sworn that the faintest shadow of a smile flickered over the woman's lips.
SH-AIK4

Arthur Ignatius Keller – The Valley of Fear – The New-York Tribune, 11th October 1914

"WATSON, WOULD YOU BE AFRAID TO SLEEP IN THE SAME ROOM WITH A LUNATIC?"

Image 5/11. Page 9. "Watson, would you be afraid to sleep in the same room with a lunatic?"
SH-AIK5

"We were aware of a man who seemed to have emerged from the wall."

Image 6/11. Page 10-11. "We were aware of a man who seemed to have emerged from the wall."
SH-AIK6

Arthur Ignatius Keller – The Valley of Fear – The New-York Tribune, 25th October 1914

Image 7/11. Page 10-11. " 'If your heart is as big as your body, and your soul as fine as your face, then I'd ask for nothing better,' said McMurdo"
SH-AIK7

Arthur Ignatius Keller – The Valley of Fear – The New-York Tribune, 1st November 1914

Image 8/11. Page 10-11. " It was all he could do to keep himself from screaming out."
SH-AIK8

Image 9/11. Page 10-11. "Stand back!" cried McMurdo "I'll blow your face in if you lay a hand on me!"
SH-AIK9

Arthur Ignatius Keller – The Valley of Fear – The New-York Tribune, 15th November 1914

"Oh, Jack, I implore you to give it up!"

Image 10/11. Page 10-11. "Oh, Jack, I implore you give it up!"
SH-AIK10

Arthur Ignatius Keller – The Valley of Fear – The New-York Tribune, 22nd November 1914

Image 11/11. Page 10-11. "Not a sound, for your lives!" McMurdo whispered. *SH-AIK11*

First 4 volumes Index

www.ingramcontent.com/pod-product-compliance
Lightning Source LLC
Chambersburg PA
CBHW081134300726
48982CB00005B/960
* 9 7 8 1 8 0 4 2 4 0 7 6 2 *